"I'm not following you. Where is he going to move to? London? Leonard has always told me how much he hates London."

"Not that he's actually been there more than a handful of times," Alessio returned drily. "But no. London wasn't what I had in mind."

"Then where?"

"I have a place at Lake Garda in northern Italy. It's close enough to get there on my private jet in a matter of hours so the trip shouldn't be too taxing for him."

"Oh, right. Okay."

"If we plan on leaving in roughly a week's time, it will give me sufficient time to get the ball rolling with the company so that I can install some of my own people to tie up all the loose ends. I'll also have enough time for my PA to source the best crew available to get this job done here and of course, there will have to be time spent packing away anything valuable that needs to be protected. I suggest several of the more robust rooms in the West Wing would be suitable for that."

"Wait, hang on just a minute! We...?"

Cathy Williams can remember reading Harlequin books as a teenager, and now that she is writing them, she remains an avid fan. For her, there is nothing like creating romantic stories and engaging plots, and each and every book is a new adventure. Cathy lives in London, and her three daughters—Charlotte, Olivia and Emma—have always been, and continue to be, the greatest inspirations in her life.

Books by Cathy Williams

Harlequin Presents

Desert King's Surprise Love-Child
Consequences of Their Wedding Charade
Hired by the Forbidden Italian
Bound by a Nine-Month Confession
A Week with the Forbidden Greek

Secrets of the Stowe Family

Forbidden Hawaiian Nights
Promoted to the Italian's Fiancée
Claiming His Cinderella Secretary

Visit the Author Profile page
at Harlequin.com for more titles.

Cathy Williams

—

THE HOUSEKEEPER'S
INVITATION TO ITALY

HARLEQUIN
PRESENTS

HARLEQUIN®
PRESENTS™

Recycling programs
for this product may
not exist in your area.

ISBN-13: 978-1-335-73915-5

The Housekeeper's Invitation to Italy

Copyright © 2023 by Cathy Williams

Harlequin Enterprises ULC
22 Adelaide St. West, 41st Floor
Toronto, Ontario M5H 4E3, Canada
www.Harlequin.com

Printed in U.S.A.

THE HOUSEKEEPER'S INVITATION TO ITALY

To my supportive and loving daughters.

CHAPTER ONE

THE BUILDING WASN'T quite what Sophie had been expecting. Although now that she was standing outside the impressive Georgian edifice she had to concede that she had just rushed to assume the obvious.

Arrogant billionaire…shiny over-the-top offices. The sort of place that announced in no uncertain terms that its occupant was not a man to be messed with because he was bigger, stronger and richer than you.

Buffeted by a brutal winter wind, and noting that it was already dark at a little after five-thirty in the afternoon, she remained hesitantly staring at the building.

It was an impeccably groomed four-storeyed town house, fronted by black railings and a shallow flight of steps that led up to a black door. In all respects it was identical to all the other town houses in this uber-prestigious crescent in the heart of London. From Bentleys to Teslas, every single car parked was high-end. There was a hush about the place which made her think that if she hung around for too long, staring and frowning and dithering, wondering whether she had done the right thing or not, then someone would materialise out of thin air and escort her right back to the busy streets a stone's throw away. Possibly by the scruff of her neck.

Galvanised by the prospect of that, Sophie hurried across the completely empty road, up the bank of steps, and realised that the gleaming brass knocker was just there for show—because there was a discreet panel of buttons to the side and a speakerphone.

Just for a few seconds, she took time out to contemplate where she was and why.

She'd had a long and uncomfortable journey from raw and wintry Yorkshire down to London—a journey undertaken with the sort of subterfuge she personally loathed, and with an outcome that was far from predictable. She had a message to be relayed under cover of darkness, because Leonard-White had expressly banned her from contacting his son, and what sort of reception was she going to get? Having gone against the wishes of her boss to uneasily follow what her inner voice had told her?

She had no idea, because Alessio Rossi-White, from everything she had seen of him, was a forbidding and terrifyingly remote law unto himself.

Sophie pressed the buzzer, and the nerves which she had been keeping at bay leapt out from their hiding places and her heart began to beat faster. The disembodied voice on the other end was a woman's, clipped and well-modulated, and it told her that, no, unless an appointment had been made, there was absolutely no chance that she would be allowed in.

'I'm afraid,' the woman said, without a trace of regret in her voice, 'that Mr Rossi-White is only in the city for a few days, and his calendar is far too packed for him to see *anyone* at all, whatever the circumstances. Of course,' she added, 'if you would like to make an appointment...'

'I've spent hours getting here...'

The cut-glass accent dropped a few shades down from cool to positively glacial. 'Perhaps you should have checked first to find out whether Mr Rossi-White was available? Now, if you don't mind, I have calls waiting—'

'I *do* mind, actually,' Sophie interjected, before the next sound she heard could be the sound of a disconnected intercom. However unpleasant this task was, she was here for a reason, and she wasn't going to be deterred by a receptionist, however cut-glass the accent happened to be.

She had dealt with bigger, weightier setbacks in her life than an overprotective receptionist behind a closed door. The bottom line was that she wasn't leaving until she saw Alessio Rossi-White and told him about his father.

'I *beg* your pardon!'

'This is personal,' Sophie said shortly, unwilling to divulge anything further to someone whose business it most certainly wasn't. 'If you really want to refuse me entry, then be my guest. But I can assure you that there'll be hell to pay when Alessio finds out that I've been turned away.'

She noted the momentary hesitation at the other end of the speakerphone and quietly breathed a sigh of relief. Of course she should have done precisely as the woman advised and alerted Alessio to the fact that she was travelling to London to see him, but it had all been all so hurried and so hush-hush. She'd known he would be in London because, in her typically formal manner, his PA always uploaded his movements to his father's email on a weekly basis. Just in case. To her knowledge, Leonard had never once used the information to contact his son.

So, yes, she'd known where to pin him down, but still…it had been a time of anxiety, during which she had barely stopped to catch her breath as revelation after revelation had crawled out of the woodwork, sending her into a tailspin. It went so beyond her brief to be here that she seemed to have lost sight of her job title completely—but what else could she do? She was incredibly fond of Leonard, and the thought of the uncertainty and stress he had carried around with him for months…was still carrying…had propelled her into this unfamiliar territory. She was paid way over the odds for her work, and with that, she accepted, came unfamiliar territory—even if this category of 'unfamiliar' was something she hadn't banked on ever having to deal with.

'I'll see what I can do. Might I have your name?'

'Sophie Court.'

Would he even recognise the name?

'You can tell him that I work for his father.'

'Please hold the line.'

It took Alessio a couple of seconds to register the name, but it fell into place as soon as he was told that the woman was his father's nurse/companion.

Or maybe it was companion/nurse. It was a distinction that had never really been clarified.

His father had had a stroke two years ago—or, as he had impatiently brushed it off as, *'A silly health scare... nothing to worry about...no need to tramp all the way to Yorkshire... I might be old but I'm not completely decrepit yet...* But did he really need someone to look after him on a daily basis?

The last time Alessio had visited—which had been months previously—the old man had seemed his usual self. Scowling...impatient...and disinclined to do or say anything that went beyond the absolute minimum on the politeness scale. There had certainly been no touching confidences of any kind—not that there ever was. When it came to their quarterly duty visits, punctuated with dry, superficial telephone exchanges, he and his father had cornered the market.

Alessio had long given up debating the normality of this situation. It was what it was. If his was a life of hard edges, a place where regret and nostalgia no longer existed, then it was because bitter experience had shaped him, and he had grown to see those hard edges as symbols of an inner strength that had made him the hugely successful and powerful man he was.

Sophie Court... He'd forgotten the woman even existed. She had certainly never been in evidence on the last few occasions he had visited his father's estate.

But here she was, and she couldn't have come at a worse time, because his inbox was overburdened with things waiting to be addressed. Several meetings were banked up, and he had an overseas conference call in under an hour with three CEOs in three different time zones.

Whatever she had come to say, she would have to say it quickly, succinctly, and without any embellishments.

Time, after all, was money.

In truth, he couldn't begin to think what might require a visit from the woman, and he buzzed her up and settled back in his chair, fully prepared to dispatch her if she didn't cut to the chase in time for him to complete what remained of his already long day on schedule.

She wasn't kept waiting. For that, Sophie was relieved. Because the less time she had to think about what she had to say, the less leeway it gave her nerves to spiral away in the wrong direction.

The truth was that she could handle pretty much whatever life chose to throw at her. She was twenty-nine years old now, and from the age of fifteen, when her father had died, she had been the one to pick up the pieces, in charge of the household, with all her youthful dreams snatched away by grim, unforgiving reality.

A kid sister, five years younger, to be protected... A mother who had retreated into her own depressed world, barely able to function and certainly not able to keep things together, to be supported... And a scattering of relatives who had clucked with sympathy whilst shutting all their doors when it came to actually helping out on any kind of practical level.

Money had been scarce, and she'd had to learn fast how to run a household efficiently, with minimum resources, and how to claim what benefits could be claimed just so that they could all survive.

She had studied hard, made sure Addy kept her head down, and nursed her mother through months and years of bewildered misery. If lessons had been learnt the biggest, for Sophie, had been to avoid the recklessness of becoming so dependent on one person that your world fell apart when that person was removed from it.

Her mother had loved too much. That would never be Sophie's downfall.

Her years at school had been a grinding mix of studying hard and working at whatever after-school jobs she could pick up so that there was a little extra cash coming in. There had been a mortgage to maintain, bills to be paid, and the juggling act involved to keep all the balls in the air had made her grow up at the speed of light. There had been no time to enjoy her adolescence. Too much had been going on.

Her dream of becoming a doctor had bitten the dust but, that said, she had found joy in the nursing career she had fallen back on, and even more in working for Leonard. Because hers was far more than a simple nursing job, and it paid so well that for the first time in her life she was able to save a bit, whilst helping out her mother and her sister.

Life had been tough, but she had handled it.

Alessio Rossi-White, though...

No, he was an entity she couldn't handle. He did something to her—made the hairs on the back of her neck stand on end and sent her nervous system into disturbing freefall. She had met him only a handful of times since she had started working for his father two years ago, and she had known instantly that she would always make sure that her days off coincided with his visits.

He was cold, arrogant and dismissive. He came for the barest minimum of time and always, *always* managed to give the impression that he had better things to do. On every level, he was the most objectionable man she had ever met in her life. She didn't think he had addressed her directly once, on any of the occasions when they had met, and with his father he was cool, guarded, and so chillingly formal that he made her shiver. From opposite ends of the table they would sit and exchange information with such a lack of warmth that it was little wonder his father had absolutely prohibited her from telling his son about his ongoing problems.

She had taken matters into her own hands because she had seen no choice, but even so, she still wondered whether she was doing the right thing.

Standing outside the pristine Georgian town house had been sufficiently daunting, but inside it was even more so. Pale marble and burnished wood were complemented by a discreet scattering of exotic plants in strategic places. The desk behind which sat the woman whose mission had been to get rid of her was a masterpiece of dull chrome and highly glossed very smooth wood, and the paintings on the walls were all abstracts which looked as expensive as everything else.

There were no raised voices from above…no sounds of ringing phones and no clattering of urgent footsteps.

If vast wealth could have a sound, then this soft hush was it.

Sophie was tempted to turn tail and flee, but instead she smiled politely at the immaculately groomed thirty-something blonde before briefly taking a seat by the window.

So this was what money looked like, she thought. His Leonard's estate was huge and sprawling and grand, but inside it had remained unchanged over the years, with dated furnishings and an air of fast-fading elegance. It was a once-grand house quietly collecting dust from the lack of money being spent on it. This space, though...

She knew that it was just one of Alessio's offices and the smallest, specifically used by his massively profitable elitist hedge fund team. His other huge offices were in Rome, Lisbon and Zurich, and from there the many tentacles of all his other concerns were managed.

She was channelled into a glass elevator which whizzed her up three floors to the top and disgorged her into an area that looked more like an office, insofar as there were desks separated by wood and glass partitions, and people sitting behind those desks surrounded by screens and working with the sort of quiet, frowning concentration that seemed to indicate huge sums of money being handled.

They barely glanced at her as she walked past them.

At the very end of the open-plan space were a handful of private offices, and Alessio's was right at the end. Only when she was standing outside, hand poised to knock on the streamlined highly polished walnut door which was slightly ajar, did she feel that flutter of butterflies in her tummy once again, and this time it had nothing to do with the conversation waiting to be had. This time it had to do with the fact of *seeing* him.

It had been a while. She revived all the reasons why she disliked the man, but her stomach clenched as she was called in to an outer office by his PA, who was expecting her. She was relieved of her coat and scarf and woolly hat, and was aware of murmured pleasantries, but all she could focus on was the solid door dividing this outer office from Alessio's inner sanctum.

Did the smartly dressed PA even know who she was? Her manner was crisp, but uber polite, and Sophie assumed that, given the reach of Alessio's power, if he'd allowed her entry within his hallowed walls, then that was sufficient to ensure all due respect from every single one of his employees, whether they knew who she was or not.

He owned them all, didn't he? From what Sophie had glimpsed of the man in the past, his attitude was that of someone who owned everyone around him and really didn't mind them knowing.

She breathed in deeply, waiting for the imposing door in front of which she was standing to be opened, her heart beating in her chest like a sledgehammer as her head was suddenly filled with visions of the man she was about to confront.

Tall…olive-skinned…with raven-dark hair and even darker eyes. He was the embodiment of physical perfection, as beautiful and as cold as any marble statue ever sculpted. Every line of his half-Italian ancestry was imprinted in the aggressive, sinful perfection of his features.

Sophie had seen pictures of Isabella Rossi, his mother, who had died many years previously, and had been rendered speechless by her outrageous sultry beauty, every gene of which she had passed down to Alessio, her only child.

Everything single thing around her...the streamlined dove-grey furniture...the pale silk rug on the blonde wooden floor...the cream leather sofa tucked against the wall...faded away as that connecting door was gently pushed open and there he was, sprawled behind a desk the size of a single bed, hands folded behind his head, waiting.

There was only mild curiosity on his face as he looked at Sophie, who stood, hovering, in the centre of his massive office as the door behind her was closed.

The woman specialised in the art of fading into the background, Alessio mused. Grey trousers, grey jumper, a long dark cardigan and an over-the-shoulder bag that might have held the kitchen sink. She had short-cropped fair hair and brown eyes, and in defiance of nearly every woman he had ever met seemed to have only a passing acquaintance with make-up. And yet there was still something about her that defied the faded image she seemed intent on conveying.

He continued to stare at her in silence, vaguely trying to work out what it was about her that didn't conform to the uninspired standard she clearly wanted to set, before abruptly sitting forward, slapping the desk with both hands and nodding to the wide black leather chair in front of it.

'No need to stand by the door as if waiting for divine inspiration, Miss Court. Have a seat and tell me what you're doing here. Tea? Coffee? Something a bit more spirited?'

He glanced at his watch before rising to his feet and strolling towards the window to briefly peer outside at bleak, grey, wintry London, before spinning round to face her. He perched against the window ledge and shoved his hands in the pockets of his trousers, while she slid into the chair opposite his desk and tucked her hair neatly behind her ears.

'No, thanks.'

'Well…? I would while away some more time on pleasantries, but I'm afraid I have a lot to do…'

'Maybe I'll have a cup of coffee after all,' Sophie said. 'It's been a long trip getting here.'

She realised that she actually needed a few pleasantries before launching into what she had to say. She needed to swim in the shallows for a bit before diving into the deep end.

She looked around her, taking in her surroundings. The building might be Georgian, but it had been refurbished to a dizzyingly modern standard, with muted colours and pale chairs and cream wooden shutters at the windows.

'I didn't expect you to work in a place like this,' she heard herself say, and blushed when he raised his eyebrows in question and he lazily strolled back towards his desk. He sat, pushing the chair at an angle so that he could tilt it back, his long legs stretched to the side and crossed at the ankles. A dangerous predator at rest.

'A place like what?'

Sophie shrugged and steeled herself to meet the jet-black eyes lazily pinned to her face. 'I suppose I expected something more modern. Glass and steel.'

Hard edges for a hard man.

'This part of my business portfolio deals exclusively with hedge funds. My clients enjoy privacy, and that's exactly what they get in this postcode. I'm surprised to see you here, Sophie, but I can only assume that this has something to do with my father?'

His eyes didn't leave her face for a single second as he buzzed through to his PA and asked for a pot of coffee.

'Or are you here for some other reason?'

'No.'

What other reason could she possibly have had for visiting this guy?

'I am here about your dad... I wish I could put this another way, but Leonard had another stroke a couple of weeks ago,' she said bluntly.

She noted the way he suddenly stilled, the way his eyes narrowed and the guarded mantle that dropped over him like a powerful protective shield.

'That's impossible.'

'What do you mean?'

'I would have known.'

Coffee was brought in, but Sophie barely noticed because she was riveted by his dark, dark eyes, which were now as hard and as cold as the frozen wastes of Siberia.

She knew so much about this man—largely through all the articles his father had tucked away about him over the years, and from the pages of the memoirs he faithfully dictated every evening, just before his dinner was served. Whether she liked it or not, she knew where he worked, and what he did, and all about the fortune he had single-handedly amassed from the springboard of his mother's inheritance, bequeathed to him when she'd died many years previously.

She knew that he was some kind of financial genius. She also knew that he was a guy who played as hard as he worked. She had seen the carefully cut-out glossy pictures of him captured by paparazzi, with a series of gorgeous tiny little blondes on his arm, usually smiling and gazing up at him with adoring eyes. She knew that none of them ever stayed the course.

Now, she shivered and wondered what it was that drew all those women to him. Surely, however rich and beautiful the man was, no one could ever really be attracted to someone as chillingly cold as he was? Money talked, but surely it didn't talk *that* much?

Looking at him now, mesmerised against her will, Sophie tried and failed to imagine him laughing or crying or showing any emotion. Certainly, on the few occasions when she'd seen him with his father, none had been in evidence.

She thought of Leonard and those meticulously and lovingly collected articles about his son and she hard-

ened inside—because Alessio had certainly never re-
paid his father's devotion with any show of affection…
none that she'd ever witnessed at any rate.

'How?' she asked flatly. 'How would you have
known when you never visit?'

'I beg your pardon?'

This was the first time Sophie had ever really spoken to Alessio, aside from polite utterances in the company of his father, after which she had faded away into
the role of practically invisible carer, there to do a job
and not contribute to the conversation. Now she felt as
though there was a dam inside her, waiting to burst.

She had survived years of having to make herself
heard by people in positions of authority, which, in the
beginning, as a shy, gawky teenager, had been alien to
her. Her sister had always been the bubbly, outgoing
one, who captured attention because she was so small
and pretty, with her blonde hair and baby blue eyes. But
circumstances had foisted a personality upon Sophie
that had become ingrained. She had learned to stick
up for herself and to have a voice, and she saw no reason why she shouldn't exercise that voice now. Because
after all Alessio, for all his money and power, wasn't
the one who paid her salary, was he?

She uneasily wondered how many more pay-cheques
would be coming her way, all things considered, and
then decided that that was all the more reason to tell this
arrogant, odious guy exactly what she thought.

If she'd read him correctly, then he was the sort of
man rarely confronted by people who spoke their mind.

'The last time you came to see your father was over five months ago.'

'Do I detect a note of criticism in your voice, Miss Court?'

'I think it's amazing that you seem surprised by what I've come to say. I think it's even more amazing that you actually expect to be in the loop when it comes to your father's day-to-day life when you're hardly around.'

'I don't believe I'm hearing this!'

'I'm only being honest.'

'And remind me when I asked for your honesty?' he gritted in a voice that could freeze water, as he stared at her with grim disbelief. 'I don't believe I've ever heard you mutter more than two words at a stretch, and yet you've suddenly decided to show up here uninvited and give me the benefit of your opinions.'

Sophie flushed and met his coldly discouraging gaze head-on and with silence.

'So,' he continued icily, 'returning to the matter at hand. My father's had another stroke. When exactly did this happen, and why is this the first time I'm hearing about it?'

His dark eyes were boring into her and they never left her face—even when the door was gently opened and his PA reminded him that he was due somewhere in under half an hour as she depositing a coffee pot on his desk. He dismissed her with a couple of words and a wave of his hand, and informed her that he was not to be disturbed until he said otherwise.

He clicked his tongue impatiently when Sophie didn't immediately fill in the silence and answer his questions.

'You have a duty of care to my father,' he informed her acidly, 'and part of that duty entails informing me of all matters pertaining to his health.'

'He forbade me from doing so,' Sophie returned bluntly, and then felt awful at the sight of the dark flush that spread across his sharp cheekbones.

She'd toughened up over the years because she'd had to, but since when had she lost the ability to empathise? Alessio might rub her the wrong way, and he might have little or no time for his father, but was it really in her remit to pass judgement on anyone? To be needlessly forthright? She'd struck a nerve, and if she could have swallowed those words back then she would have.

She might have needed strength to deal with what Fate had thrown at her, but she had also needed patience, understanding and love, and she'd always had those in abundance.

Those were the very qualities that had seen her look out for her younger sister, support her in her endeavours to become an actress, even though, personally, Sophie could not have thought of a less sensible road to travel down. They were also the qualities that had guided her through her darkest moments, when her mother had been a lost soul, unable to cope after her husband's sudden death.

Both were settled now, but being tough had only been part of the answer when it had come to handling their adversities, so where had her sense of sympathy gone?

'I'm sorry,' she said quietly. 'I shouldn't have said that.'

'Because it's not true?'

'It was a tactless way of putting it and I can see that I've hurt you.'

Alessio stiffened. *Hurt?* He was incapable of being hurt. He had been hurt in the past—hurt by the death of his beloved mother, hurt by the indifference of his father towards him in the aftermath of that death. Dealing with those past hurts had toughened him...made him impregnable. His lips thinned in affront that the woman sitting opposite him might actually think herself capable of hurting him by anything she said.

He felt as though he might be seeing Sophie Court for the very first time, because on those other occasions she had been as quiet as a mouse, head bowed, voice subdued when he'd addressed her, with none of the fire on display now.

For the first time in a long time, he was discovering what it felt like to be in the presence of the unexpected. She might be dressed like a maiden aunt, but she certainly wasn't behaving like one, and he narrowed his eyes and looked at her...*really* looked at her.

Tall, slender, she had skin as pale as alabaster and a wary expression in her brown eyes that spoke of a contained personality.

Why was she so contained? And how was it that someone still in her twenties was willing to take on the full-time role of looking after an old, cantankerous man?

A sudden wave of curiosity threatened to steal a march, and he brought it firmly back to heel.

'Don't worry about my feelings, Miss Court,' he said with exaggerated politeness. 'I've always found that I'm perfectly capable of handling them myself. So my father would rather I did not know of his stroke? He's proud and likes to think he's infallible. Sadly, he's not. What has his consultant said?'

He decided to refrain from telling her that not only should she have immediately told him what had happened, but should also have ensured that he was kept in the loop by his father's consultant.

'Well?' he prompted, when he was greeted with silence.

He felt the stirrings of disquiet. So much water had flowed under that bridge, so many doors had been shut over the years, and yet the thought of losing his father was oddly unsettling. Was it because there had been so many issues that had never been addressed by either of them?

His heart picked up pace and he suddenly sprang to his feet to pace the room, walking jerkily to the window and staring out at the private circular courtyard, which was lit enough for him to make out the exquisite landscaping, the hedges and overhanging trees, the vague shapes of the benches where his employees could choose to relax whenever they wanted.

'Is he in a critical condition?' Alessio demanded, raking his fingers through his hair as he spun round to face her.

'He was in hospital for two nights. He's back home now.'

Alessio breathed a sigh of relief. 'Then why this reticence on the subject? You should know that the last time my father had a stroke he waved aside my offers to go to Glenn House, so he has form when it comes to making sure his pride takes precedence over everything.'

Looking at him, Sophie was startled at the bitterness that had crept into his voice. Was he even aware of it?

'The consultant said that the stroke was very likely caused by stress.'

'What has my father got to be stressed about?' Alessio asked, his voice genuinely puzzled.

'He's been having financial worries.'

'I would know if that were true. We don't talk a great deal, but we do cover the financial markets. He would have said something. No. You must be mistaken.' He sighed. 'This is not the right place to be having a conversation of this nature.'

'It doesn't matter where we are,' Sophie told him. 'I'll just say what I've come to say and then I'll leave.'

'It's nearly six-thirty. Have you eaten today at all? What time did you leave Harrogate?'

He was talking and walking, and Sophie watched in consternation as he began putting on his jacket and then opened a concealed door that faded into the polished walnut panels to extract a coat.

'I know a wine bar not a million miles away. We can go there. I think I might need a drink for this particular conversation.'

'What about your work? Your meetings?'

Did she *want* to carry on chatting in a wine bar? She

was uncomfortable with the idea of that. Maybe even a little panicked, although she wasn't entirely sure why.

She could understand why he might find it constricting to have an intensely personal conversation with interruptions from his PA and his computer reminding him that there was still work to be done, even though in most normal offices the stampede for the exit would have already begun. It was late, and yet there were no signs that anyone was getting ready to leave. She figured that making money didn't keep nine-to-five hours. A bit like nursing.

'I'm the boss,' he said neutrally, coming to stand directly in front of her, his towering six-foot-three swamping her senses and bringing her out in a fine nervous perspiration. 'The buck stops with me. If I want to cancel meetings, I can do it. The position of tycoon,' he said, with wry self-mockery, 'comes with little perks like that.'

Just like that, Sophie felt her breath leave her in a whoosh and she glanced away quickly, although she could feel the heat in her face as he continued to look at her for a few more seconds before moving away.

She stood up, but her mind was all over the place as she reached for her bag. She'd come with a prepared speech, and all she could think was that she'd somehow been swept away on an unexpected riptide that had not at all been part of her plan.

In no corner of her mind had she anticipated being ushered into a chauffeur-driven Bentley, staring out from behind privacy glass at pedestrians scurrying across packed pavements, and then being swept into a wine bar that was the last word in understated mono-chrome luxury, with black leather sofas and stark wooden floors and concrete effect walls.

For the whole of the trip Alessio had been on his phone, sometimes switching languages, making sure that his work was covered in his unplanned absence from the office.

It had been a relief, because it had given her time to get her scattered thoughts in order and to remind herself that this was, in essence, a business conversation. Nothing she couldn't handle.

You can do this, and before you know it, it'll be another day...

It was the mantra she had repeated to herself so many times through the years, as her adolescence had slipped away between her fingers, lost in the business of growing up too fast.

She repeated it now, as she perched on the edge of the plush leather sofa, but even so she still tensed when he leaned towards her from his chair opposite, dwarfing the thin glass table separating them, and said in a low, driven undertone, 'So, Miss Court, here we are. Time to talk to me about everything that's been going on with my father. You have my undivided attention...'

CHAPTER TWO

UP CLOSE TO HER, as he was now, Alessio absently noted that she had the most unusual eyes—almond-shaped and nut-brown and fringed with very long, dark lashes, dramatic against the smooth pallor of her skin. His eyes drifted to the stern, no-nonsense cropped hair. He was so accustomed to women advertising their assets that this particular woman's strenuous efforts to disguise what she had under her drab, unrevealing clothes roused a flare of curiosity.

Just briefly.

'Well?' he prompted. 'You've decided that a character assassination is in order, so the very least you could do now is tell me what exactly I've been assassinated for. You've told me that my father's stroke may have been caused by stress, and you've followed that up with hints about money problems he's been having. Money problems I know nothing about because, of course, I am the son who doesn't give a damn. So I think a little more enlightenment is in order, don't you?'

He sat back when a waiter approached, but instead of taking the menus extended he ordered tapas, leaving the selection up to the chef, and a bottle of Chablis. Not once did his eyes leave her face.

'Or,' he drawled, as she chewed her lip and met his unwavering dark gaze with silence, 'have you got more criticisms of me stashed up your sleeve before you cut to the chase and get down to providing me with a little proof to back up what you're saying? Please...' he waved his arms expansively '...don't let good manners stand in the way of home truths.'

Sophie was sorely tempted to tell him that, yes, she had lots more criticism stashed up her sleeve, but instead she snapped out of her dazed silence and pursed her lips.

'The two things are connected,' she said quietly. 'Your father's health and the fact that he has financial problems. He didn't want you to know about either of them, but I felt I had no choice but to tell you because his bank manager paid a visit to the house while he was in hospital and confided in me that most of the company holdings are in the red. I don't know the exact details, but I gather a loan was taken out against the company some years ago and repayment is now being demanded—except there's nothing to pay it back with because the company has been losing money for years. I think Mr Ellis would have contacted you directly, but he's always been under strict instructions that all financial matters are to be kept private and under no circumstances are you to be asked to intervene. I think the only reason he spoke to me was because he felt he had no choice.'

'He felt he had *no choice*? I don't believe I'm hearing this...' Alessio muttered under his breath. 'What the hell has the old fool been getting up to up to behind my back?'

'Don't say that,' Sophie returned, stricken. 'He's proud. Many people his age are. He admires you so much and he doesn't want you to find out that he's made mistakes and... I don't know...trusted people to do a job which they haven't done...'

Alessio laughed humourlessly. 'I suggest you stick to the script, Miss Court, and not go off-piste with yet more personal observations that bear no resemblance to reality. It's outrageous that Ellis didn't come to me first.'

'I suppose client confidentiality...'

'And yet you're here, despite my father forbidding you to get in touch with me.'

'I care about him very much, and I don't think he can survive the collapse of his company.'

'I'll need to get full details of whatever mess my father has got himself into. And Ellis should start scouring the job columns, because when I'm through with him he'll realise just how misjudged his loyalties have been.'

'How can you be so unsympathetic?' Sophie gasped, as impulse got the better of common sense.

'If you think this is the sound of me being unsympathetic, then stick around and you'll find out what it *really* sounds like when my patience snaps,' Alessio grated. 'I'm being practical. Ellis is a bank manager. He's in charge of money matters. He's not there for hand-wringing and misplaced loyalties. When it comes to bankruptcy, all's fair in love and war. The man should not have thought twice about coming to me. Who else can sort out my father's financial problems? Magic fairies with chequebooks? If I'd known about these money problems earlier, they would have been sorted by now.'

They were interrupted by the arrival of food, but for a couple of seconds Sophie was barely aware of the dishes being placed on the table in front of them because she was one hundred per cent mesmerised by the eyes pinned to her face. The man was hypnotic and terrifying in equal measure.

'I don't know all the ins and outs…'

'You know enough, and I'm guessing that if you think it's drastic enough to bring yourself out of hiding to confront me here, then chances are it's even worse than you imagine.'

'I haven't been in hiding.'

'I can't think of the last time I set eyes on you when I was at my father's house.'

'I… I like to leave you both to…to bond. You don't need me hovering in the background, dishing out Leonard's tablets and telling him what he can and can't eat…'

'You'd be surprised. It might make a refreshing variation on our usual line of conversation, which would appear to be even more superficial than I thought possible if he's been keeping all of this from me. But enough of that. First and foremost, do *you* need help.'

'Help…?'

'On a practical level. Someone to assist with my father's recovery now he's at home. I realise you're a qualified nurse, but there might be issues with physically helping my father to move around that you might find tricky on your own.'

Sophie was impressed by his immediate grasp of what might be necessary. He was being practical, and she realised that in a strange way that was just what she needed, because her emotions had been running wild for the past few days. Focusing on the more pedestrian stuff would calm her, and having someone else alongside her in doing that would be even more calming, even if the 'someone' in question was Alessio.

There was also concern in his voice. She could *sense* it. And yet on the surface anyone would think that he was dealing with a business matter, without the intrusion of any emotions muddying the water. She'd presented him with a problem and he was finding ways to deal with it, because he was solution-orientated.

'No...' She paused, then added with heartfelt honesty, 'But thanks for asking and I mean that.' She half smiled and belatedly began to pick at the tapas, because she was ravenous. 'You'd be surprised how strong you need to be when you're a nurse. There's a lot of lifting involved, but we're all trained in how to do it in the most efficient and least damaging way possible.'

'What else do you do?' Alessio asked abruptly, and Sophie looked at him with surprise.

'What do you mean?'

'You're...how old?'

'Twenty-nine,' she said awkwardly.

'You're twenty-nine years old and yet you're content to work full-time for my father. He hasn't needed round-the-clock care for all these years, surely. So, that being the case, what do you *do*? You're young. Don't you find the work lacking in stimulation?'

Sophie stiffened. His voice was genuinely curious, and that was what made it all the more insulting.

Twenty-nine years old and willing to spend most of her days with an old man. An old and very interesting man, but an old man all the same. And she had more than sufficient time off, and saw her nursing friends as often as she could, catching them when they weren't on awkward shifts…having a laugh with them and watching from the sidelines as they all began to get involved in serious relationships.

That was a world she was not tempted to enter. She'd seen what love could do. She wasn't her mother—of course not. She hoped she had more inner strength. But who knew? She couldn't bear to think about losing herself in anyone to the point where she became so reliant on them that if they were snatched away her life would collapse into pieces.

Was that being wise and cautious? Or had she become accustomed to running scared? She didn't know. Maybe she would go there one day, but it would be with someone who was more of a friend…someone who wouldn't get to her enough to topple her world if things didn't work out.

Was she content to work for an old man because, subconsciously, it prevented her from tackling the real world and dipping her toes into the unpredictable business of dating? Her last boyfriend had been a nice guy, but they had broken up years previously. He had wanted more than she was capable of giving. Was that to be her destiny?

It didn't scare her. Never finding true love didn't scare her. Finding it and losing it did.

Still, those mildly curious eyes on her were unsettling.

'Is it any less stimulating than working behind a computer in an office?' she retorted sharply, her bristles up.

She was uncomfortably aware that she'd thought nothing of telling him what she thought of him, and yet now she was resentful and defensive because he was repaying the favour. He'd struck a nerve without even realising it.

'I… I'm not held prisoner at your father's house,' she expanded, talking into a silence that was getting on her nerves. 'I see a lot of my friends who are in the nursing profession.'

'And you don't miss being out there with them?'

Sophie paused, but only fractionally. 'They're rushed off their feet all the time,' she said truthfully. 'They work shifts and they don't get paid enough.'

'You *are* extremely well-compensated,' Alessio murmured, tilting his head to one side and pushing his plate away with one finger, so that he could relax back in his chair. 'Money means a lot to you?' He leaned forward again, voice low, eyes coolly assessing. 'Underneath the care and concern, have you come here to tell me about my father's financial situation because you fear you could lose your job if there's no money to pay you?'

'No!' She felt the sting of colour in her cheeks.

But wasn't the money more or less essential? She was paid a small fortune compared to all her friends, and that money disappeared down the drain. She helped her sister out, because acting jobs were few and far between and the temp work Addy did so that she could go to auditions at the drop of a hat didn't pay very much. And of course there was her mother…now living in Somerset with the family home sold. But there was still a mortgage, and someone had to pay it. Thank goodness it was small.

'Where are you staying?' he queried in an abrupt change of subject.

Sophie blinked and stared at him in silence for a few seconds, before naming a cheap chain hotel in a reasonably seedy part of South-west London.

'It's all I could afford,' she blurted out when he frowned, which only made his frown deepen.

'Surely not? I don't believe that. Like I said, I happen to know how much you're paid.'

'How do you know that?'

'I insisted on handling the matter and paying the salary. I wanted to make sure my father didn't decide to get rid of you on the spur of the moment.'

'I wasn't aware…'

'Why would you be? I recognised at the time that he needed help after his first stroke. He insisted on choosing the right candidate himself, and I wanted to make sure that whoever got the job would be paid enough that he or she would think twice about leaving. My father, I imagine, isn't the easiest of people to handle.'

'He's a pussycat,' Sophie inserted absently, dwelling

on what he had said about being responsible for her pay-cheque and wishing she hadn't been so quick to speak her mind when she'd confronted him.

'Come again?'

'I had no idea you paid me.'

'Pussycat?'

'We get on like a house on fire—which is why I'm still with him, I guess. He does need some help…reminders with his diet and his medication, and making sure he does appropriate levels of exercise every day… but it's also about companionship. He all but gave up work when he had his stroke…his confidence took a knocking and he delegated everything to his CEOs. He needs companionship, even though he would never say it in so many words. And aside from my expected list of duties on the medical side of things I've also started helping him collate material for his memoirs… I drive him to places as well. He enjoys his chess club on a Wednesday, and every so often he has friends over, and is very particular about what gets served for supper…'

Listening to her, seeing the way her features softened, Alessio felt as though he was being given a glimpse of a world he knew nothing about.

Since when had his irascible, overbearing, prickly and difficult father ever been described as a *pussycat*?

And hadn't he always scorned people who played chess? Played games of any description?

Alessio could remember trundling down to his father's study, chess board under his arm, and knocking on the door behind which he had retreated following the death of his wife. Alessio had been ten at the time, and with his mother only gone a handful of weeks the loneliness of his bedroom had become too much.

But his father didn't play games. That much Alessio remembered very clearly. He didn't play games and he had no time for a child whose bedroom was too lonely or whose heart had suddenly been torn out.

Alessio had shrugged and left.

'So my money,' he drawled now, shutting the door on memories that had no place in the present, 'is at least well spent. Which brings me back to why you can't afford anywhere more salubrious to stay—especially when you could have charged it to my father's account. Or were you afraid that he might spot your destination and have a hissy fit if he suspected you might be trundling down here to see me? No matter. You'll be pleased to hear that your contract continues to be safe.'

He called for the bill with a barely-there nod of his head.

'If I'm to intervene in my father's affairs, then he's going to have to find out that you've told me what's going on.'

'I know,' Sophie said jaggedly. 'You might want me to carry on there, but that won't be up to you if your father decides he can't trust me.'

'And what would you do should that be the outcome?' Alessio asked, his dark eyes watchful and his long, lush lashes shielding his expression.

Sophie shrugged her narrow shoulders, but she looked awkward, and a tinge of pink touched her cheeks. 'I'll do what I've always done. I'll manage.'

'You'll do what you've always done…?' he murmured.

'Don't we all?' Sophie added quickly.

Alessio looked at her steadily. In the space of a couple of hours his life had been turned on its head. From a standpoint of historical non-involvement with his father, he was now looking at a completely different picture. He would naturally have to step in and find out what the hell had been going on with his father's financial affairs, and the old man wasn't going to like that. He would also have to protect this woman who looked as though the skies had fallen in.

She needed the money. Why? And what had she meant when she'd said that she would do what she'd always done and 'manage' if she lost her job? He had no idea, and in the wider scheme of things he didn't care. It was just a miracle that someone existed who described his father as a *pussycat*.

If his father was in trouble on both fronts, with his health and with his finances, and if she was right in reporting what the consultant had said about stress being the root of his stroke, then Alessio couldn't afford to add to the stress levels.

Along with this analytical dissection of the situation Alessio felt a thread of ancient hurt trickle through him—the same hurt he had felt as a child, when his juvenile overtures after his mother's death had been met with cold rejection. Hurt that he had not been told of momentous things happening in his father's life.

He gritted his teeth and dismissed that passing weakness.

'I'll make sure to be discreet in my enquiries. I'll

get to the bottom of whatever's been going on, but my theory is mismanagement. From the little I glimpsed of my father's holdings ten years ago, it's run along the lines of a gentlemen's club—which might have worked back in the day, but doesn't cut it in this day and age.'

'Can I ask you something?'

'Would it deter you if I said *no*?' Alessio asked coolly, yet with a trace of amusement in his voice.

'How is it that you never took an interest in your father's company?'

The question lodged between them like a rock hurled into still waters. Her eyes were clear and curious, her head tilted to one side.

Alessio realised that he was in the presence of a woman who breached all boundaries. She had asked him an intensely personal question without any hint of an agenda behind the asking. She wasn't trying to get close to him. She wasn't trying to forge any kind of intimate connection by enticing confidences. She was curious and that was the end of it.

He wondered if that was why he said, surprising himself, 'My father and I…we've had a difficult relationship. My mother died when I was very young. Just ten. Things were rocky. By the time I hit twenty-one and finished my university career at Oxford, I knew that I was going to make my own way in the world without the help of my father. Fortuitously, my mother brought her own personal fortune to my parents' marriage, and much of it remained intact when she died. It was passed on to me. I suppose you could say that I had a head start when it came to getting my career going. A head start that completely bypassed my father, which suited me.'

Sophie, listening intently, nodded. 'It's good to be independent,' she murmured. 'It's good not to rely on anyone for anything.'

'You're more than welcome to ditch the cheap motel and stay at my place,' Alessio volunteered, appreciating the brevity of her response and startled by his unexpected foray into touchy-feely sharing, which was a gene he'd thought he had been born without.

But she shook her head without hesitation. 'I'm fine. Can you tell me…what happens now?'

'I'll call Ellis first thing tomorrow—and don't worry, I'll make sure no feathers are ruffled in the process. I'll get the loan that's outstanding paid off, and then I'll get my team to examine the accounts of his company in forensic detail. I'll weed out the dross, replace it with people who know that they'll be answering to me, and set things back on the straight and narrow.'

'And all of this without your father finding out what's going on?'

'Nothing is beyond the wit of man.'

'How can you achieve all that when you don't really talk to your father, Mr…er… Rossi-White?'

'I think, given the circumstances, we can dispense with the formal titles, don't you, Sophie? You can all me Alessio.'

He paused. For all the time she had been working for his father, he realised that he knew precious little about her, and it was ironic that his newly born voyage of discovery into her thoughts had kicked off by her revealing the fact that she didn't approve of him and didn't like him very much—if at all.

'Well, all things considered, it seems that I'll have to have a conversation with him now, doesn't it?' A dark flush delineated his sharp cheekbones and he shifted in the chair.

'Let's hope the sudden shock of that doesn't cause another stroke…' she said at once.

Their eyes met and Alessio burst out laughing. The laughter soon died, but his dark eyes remained on her face and he knew there was amused appreciation in them.

'Is that why you don't like me?' he drawled. 'Because you think I'm to blame for the distance that exists between me and my father?'

Just like that the atmosphere shifted.

And that was what raced through Sophie's head as she stared at him, mesmerised by the depths of his dark eyes. Some tiny voice inside was telling her that this drowning feeling carried a thread of danger.

Drowning was always about a loss of control, and she'd been there and experienced it enough to know that she was never going to return to that place again. She'd felt the panicked confusion of circumstances running away with her, pulling her in directions she couldn't handle.

She'd known real fear for her future, for her sister's future, as she'd swum in the turbulent waters of social services and GPs and school governors in the wake of her father's death, when her mother had retreated into herself with no interest in anything outside. For weeks and months treading water had become a way of life, and even when at last her mother had shaken herself out of her stupor she had still been too depressed to really engage in all sorts of small, daily decisions. Little by little she had come to, had re-entered the world, and she had never stopped apologising for leaving her daughter to handle everything on her own when she'd been just a child, too young for the responsibility. But by then Sophie had grown up, and she had seen the ugly side of losing control and what it could do to a person.

So now…

No…this drowning feeling wasn't good, but surely there was nothing to fear? This was just some silly reaction to a guy—nothing that could have any impact on her life.

Alessio got under her skin for a lot of reasons, and she had to concede that the way he looked had something to do with her reaction. She might have her head very firmly screwed on, but she was still a woman, after all, and for all his faults he was an extremely beautiful man. Who wouldn't shiver in the presence of physical perfection?

Honestly, what was there to worry about just because she was a little unsettled by those fabulous dark eyes and that exquisite bone structure? She was beyond temptation on that front—of that she was one hundred per cent sure.

Self-control regained, she said, matter-of-factly, 'I don't have any feelings for you one way or the other, and it's not something I've given much thought to.'

'Is that right?' Alessio mused with cool neutrality, eyebrows raised. 'There have been times when I've thought that you might have been actively avoiding me by making sure you weren't around on the occasions I came to see my father... That's probably a wild flight of imagination on my part...' He paused and then carried on, in the same musing, thoughtful voice, 'Although let's not forget you *did* have a lot to say on the matter when you confronted me earlier this evening...'

Sophie pursed her lips, but remained silent until he shrugged and sat back.

'No matter. All finished here? Dessert? A stiff drink for the road? No?' He signalled for the bill and looked at her from under lush lashes. 'You may have got away with scuttling out of sight like a timid little crab whenever I've been to visit before...but things are going to be a little different for a while...'

Sophie resented his phraseology, but she couldn't take issue with it because the wretched man was spot-on.

'How so?' she asked.

'Well, once I've started the business of finding out what's been going on with my father's holdings I'm going to have to be on site, to make sure everything is being done my way. I don't see any choice in the matter. His head office is based in Harrogate and I'm going to want to oversee what happens there.'

'What...? Why?'

'Like I said, there will be a need to clear the dross, and very often dross doesn't particularly like to be cleared. It's something I won't be able to delegate—at least not at ground zero. Aside from which…' He hesitated and flushed. 'My father and I may not have seen eye to eye on a range of things over the years, and he may rant and rail against my being there and seeing him when he's weak, but he's still my flesh and blood. And this time I intend to make sure his pride doesn't get in the way of my presence.'

He grimaced.

'You might have to warn him of my impending arrival, though. Like you say, the shock of an unexpected visit might spark another stroke…'

'I will. Okay…'

'Tell him that I phoned you to find out how he was because I'd heard on the grapevine that there might be problems with his company. The world of business can be small, and I am exceptionally high-profile. A lot of people know who I am and who my father is. It would only have taken one concerned voice to propel me to Harrogate… Feel free to tell him that I bullied the truth out of you about his stroke. He'll buy that easily enough.'

'Because he thinks you're a bully?' Sophie asked.

'Like I said,' Alessio drawled, 'we've had our differences over the years. He can be stubborn, and sometimes the only way to trump stubborn is to go one step further and be even more stubborn. My father may think he's tough as old boots, but he ain't seen nothing yet. I have some things to finalise here, but first thing tomorrow I'll get my people to start going through my father's accounts. I'll be up on Saturday, which will give you two days to brace him for the inevitable. If you don't think that you're up to the task, you can always give me a call…you have my number. I can always think of something to absolve you of the duty. Because you might find that my *pussycat* father can turn very easily into a roaring lion if he thinks you haven't done what he's asked you to do.'

Sophie met his gaze steadily. 'It may not be a great job, breaking the news to your dad that I've told you about his health issues, but you don't have to worry that I'm going to run scared. I won't.' She set her jaw at a stubborn angle, remembering a past stuffed with doing uncomfortable things. 'Believe me, I've dealt with my fair share of uncomfortable and unpleasant tasks.'

She blinked, smiled, smoothing away the sharp edges of what she had just said. because confiding in anyone about her past wasn't something she usually did.

'It'll be fine. Deep down, I'm sure he'll be really thrilled to see you.'

Alessio gave nothing away as he looked at her for a few seconds, digesting what she had just said. He thought absently that there was no way he would bet a buck on, that because the last thing his father was going to be thrilled by was his son's arrival on the scene with a suitcase packed for more than just a brief overnight stay.

You couldn't teach an old dog new tricks, and that particular old dog had learnt the trick of making sure that he, Alessio, knew just where his place was in the grand scheme of things.

Mostly, though, his mind was preoccupied with those 'uncomfortable and unpleasant' tasks Sophie had men-

tioned. Had she known how transparent her face had
been when she'd said that? Whatever had been flitting
through her head had cast a shadow over her features.
Maybe things to do with work? Nursing would have
brought her into close contact with a lot of uncomfortable and unpleasant tasks... But somehow he'd got
the impression that that passing remark harked back to
something that was a lot more personal.

What? Never one to delve into the quagmire of other
people's psychological motivations—because what was
the point of that?—Alessio couldn't stop another sudden flare of curiosity about the woman sitting opposite
him, so calm on the surface. And yet beneath that surface the promise of turbulence swirled...

Turbulence and passion. Didn't the two go hand in
hand?

He banked down whatever obscure wild imaginings
were trying to worm their way to the surface of his
thoughts, but he couldn't resist a second look at her
face. Alessio was accustomed to women who kept nothing hidden from him. They flung themselves at him.
They wanted him to be curious about them...to want
to get to know them. They were specialists in the art
of using their womanly wiles to get what they wanted.
They pouted and flirted, ever keen to engage his attention and hold it.

But this woman...

She had spent so long fading into the background,
or else being completely missing in action, that he had
somehow failed to notice just how flawlessly smooth

her skin was and how alluring the depth of her cool, intelligent brown eyes.

'At any rate,' he said smoothly, 'you know where to find me. You have my personal number—the one I gave you some time ago for emergency use. Use it.'

Bill paid, he stood up, and she hurriedly followed suit. His eyes drifted over her once again in casual inspection.

She was very slender. Tall and willowy. That much he could make out under the formidably dull clothes. She was wearing workmanlike flat shoes, and in them she was only a few inches shorter than him. He usually went out with small, voluptuous blondes, so it made a change to be with a woman almost at eye level with him.

But then he quickly reminded himself that this wasn't a date and he wasn't going out with the woman.

'How are you getting back to your motel?' asked Alessio.

'It's a *hotel*,' Sophie corrected, as their coats were brought and she manoeuvred herself into hers. 'Motels…motels are things in horror movies.'

She said this in an attempt to squash her previous unguarded remark about not being able to afford anything pricey. Her personal life wasn't open for perusal, so why should he know about her money issues?

Alessio shot her a curling smile. 'A sense of humour? I like it. That's a side of you that's been kept under wraps… Feel free to bring it out of hiding whenever you want while I'm around.'

Sophie blushed, momentarily lost for words. Because

this man and being light-hearted weren't things that went together in her head.

Before she could come up with a suitable response, he said, with a return to cool gravity, 'I'll probably be there for a week, depending on how things go. You'll need to put whatever issues you have with me on the back burner.'

'I have no issues with you.'

'Whether you do or don't is immaterial.' Alessio shrugged his response. 'The key thing at this stage is my father's recovery and sorting out his business problems. When those two things are dealt with…well, life will return to normal and you can…' he raised his brows and met her eyes steadily '…return to hiding from me whenever I show up. In the meanwhile, for the sake of my father, we pretend that everything is as it should be between the two of us. Agreed?'

Sophie hesitated, but only for a split-second. Alessio in close proximity for a week? But he would be occupied in dealing with all manner of things, and she would be as well. Their paths would probably cross for the barest amount of time. Could she deal with that for the sake of Leonard? Of course she could. Like Alessio said, once things were sorted he'd be off, and her life would resume where it had left off.

She nodded. 'Agreed.'

CHAPTER THREE

'YOU'RE LATE.'

That wasn't what Sophie had meant to say. What she had meant to say was: *You're a little later than expected and your father has retired to bed. He tires easily these days.*

Unfortunately, she had had an hour and a half to stew in her own frazzled nerves, and by the time the doorbell had rung, she'd been wired. She'd been wired since her trip to London.

Nothing had prepared her for meeting Alessio face to face. Yes, she'd been in his presence before, when he'd blown in from London on one of his whirlwind visits, bringing with him a sense of high-voltage energy, restless impatience and those critical dark eyes that had made her cringe. On such occasions, before she'd resorted to taking her days off in advance of his arrivals, it had been easy to mumble some pleasantries and fade into the background. As he had remorselessly pointed out when she had gone to see him.

But up close and personal with him, she had felt her nerves go into free fall. He was so much more compelling than she had given him credit for. So much more devastatingly impressive. So much more downright scary.

Those fabulous dark eyes had mesmerised her. His deep, velvety voice had wrapped around her in a stranglehold that had turned her brain to mush and left her feeling hot and bothered. By nature, she was cool, calm and collected. She had learned from a young age that common sense trumped emotion when it came to getting things done, and those lessons had stayed with her...had become part of her DNA. So it had been alarming to discover how easily all her cool could be shot to smithereens by a guy she had successfully managed to avoid for over two years.

Even more alarming had been the way her heart had beat faster in his presence, and the way her mind had started playing tricks on her, conjuring up all sorts of thoughts of Alessio as a man and not just as someone objectionable she was being forced to do business with.

There was no place in her life for such foolishness. Really, Sophie had no time for flights of fancy. Until now, they hadn't even been on her radar. Her teenage years had passed by in a fog of duty and obligation and responsibility. When all her friends had been having their adolescent flights of fancy, she had been way too focused on the nitty-gritty of taking care of her mother to follow their lead.

It had never bothered her.

In fact, hadn't she felt just a tiny bit smug when those flights of fancy had so often ended up crashing and burning?

So her meeting with Alessio had left her feeling on edge, and more so as the time of his arrival had got closer and closer.

'Damn boy could at least have the common decency to show up on time if he's to lecture to me about my business problems!' Leonard had bellowed, as he'd made his way up to his bedroom on the stairlift which had been installed two years previously.

'Traffic…' Sophie had murmured soothingly.

Which had met with a predictable, *'Pah! Traffic, schmaffic.'*

She hadn't ventured further into dangerous terrain by prolonging the conversation. The less stress Leonard had the better, and he had been on tenterhooks ever since she had broached the conversation about Alessio coming to discuss his financial situation.

It had been a blessing that he hadn't been more incandescent when she'd told him that his son had found out about his money woes and had informed her that he would be visiting so that he could discuss the situation.

She had tiptoed around the issue with the agility of someone avoiding landmines, and she had shrewdly guessed that Leonard might be privately relieved to have everything out in the open, pride or no pride.

But since Leonard had been settled in bed, tablets taken and hot drink duly brought up, Sophie had had plenty of time to fulminate.

Now, staring at Alessio, she felt all the dispassionate responses she had rehearsed vanish under a blizzard of anger.

Against the bitter wintry darkness outside, with the

raw cold of Yorkshire at its most brutal and a freezing blast of ice-cold wind tousling his hair, the man still managed to look unfairly sexy.

He was wearing a beige cashmere coat and a black scarf and, from what she could see as she blinked into the grim black night outside, dark jeans and some kind of dark jumper.

'It's only a little after nine-thirty.' Alessio brushed past her, divesting himself of his coat and scarf before turning to look at her as she slammed the front door shut against the freezing cold. 'I had no idea lights went out here at sunset.'

Sophie folded her arms, her whole body rigid with pent-up tension, already frustrated with herself for the way she was reacting to him.

'Your father retires early to bed now.'

'How early?'

'By eight he's flagging.'

'I spoke to his consultant and got a briefing on all his health issues,' Alessio said, heading towards the kitchen.

Sophie pelted behind him.

The house was enormous. They went past several rooms, most unused and all decorated in a style that had once been elegant but now seemed stuffy and over-done. The kitchen, though, which was the heart of the place—especially since Leonard had had his stroke—was warm and inviting, with a comfortable arrange-ment of sofas at one end, where French doors opened out onto the extensive gardens at the back. Right now those acres of land were shrouded in darkness.

'You were right,' said Alessio. 'The less stress he has, the better. And as an aside, I had some urgent business to conclude—hence my slightly late arrival.' He looked at her and shoved his hands in the pockets of his jeans. 'There was no need to wait up. I do actually have a key to the house, even if I don't always choose to use it.'

'I… I'm always up at this hour, Mr…er… Alessio. I was just disappointed because your father was…'

'Sorry to have missed me? I'm not buying it.' Alessio's eyebrows shot up. 'Now, I haven't eaten since this morning…' He glanced around the kitchen, and then made a slower and more thorough visual tour of his surroundings. 'If you stick around while I get myself something to eat, we can outline how this week is going to progress.'

Sophie didn't have to say anything, because it was clear that he'd assumed she would fall in line with his plans.

He began rummaging in the fridge, frowning, half bent over as he searched and sifted through the contents.

'What are you looking for?' Sophie asked politely.

Alessio glanced across at her for a couple of seconds, then resumed his search. 'Something interesting that can be stuck between two slices of bread.'

Sophie clicked her tongue impatiently and padded towards the cupboards. Then she nodded for him to sit down.

'I'll make something,' she said. 'If you'd turned up on time, you could have had dinner when we did.'

'Where did you put the leftovers?'

'In the bin. On your father's instructions.'

Alessio burst out laughing. 'Yes, that sounds about right. So, tell me… What was his response when you spun your merry little yarn about me finding out through the grapevine that his business was in trouble? Told him that I contacted you to elicit information rather than confront him directly? Or does the food being chucked in the bin say it all?'

'He was upset.' Sophie began making a ragout of tomatoes and vegetables. She was a good cook. She'd had years to get it right. 'But…' She turned to Alessio thoughtfully, running her hand through her short fair hair, spiking it up 'But I think, deep down, his ranting and railing hid a certain amount of relief. He's been carrying the burden on his shoulders alone, and that's not an easy thing to do.'

'No…' Alessio sat at the kitchen table, swivelling one of the heavy wooden chairs to face her so that he could stretch out his long legs. 'And my father is not known for his ability to bear burdens alone for very long.'

'What does that mean?'

Alessio looked at her in silence for a moment. Leonard? Coping with burdens on his own? What a joke.

He breathed in sharply, accosted by a blast from the past. A memory of that very moment when he'd been told that his father was remarrying.

Three months after his mother had died he had been dispatched off to boarding school, and six months after he'd gone there he'd been called in to the principal's office and told that he would be given two days' leave so that he could attend his father's wedding.

Alessio could remember the surge of shock and hatred that had flowed through him like toxic lava when he'd been told that.

His beloved mother had barely been buried and his father was remarrying. He had been old enough to reach conclusions he had never voiced. Had his father been having an affair all along? His mother had died in a car accident. What had she been driving away from? He had thought them to have been in love…happily married. Yes, his father had always been taciturn, and his mother a ray of joyful sunshine, filled with the sort of Italian *joie de vivre* that could light up a room. But had there been cracks he hadn't seen?

Certainly his father had changed after her death, had withdrawn into himself, but had he simply withdrawn because of guilt? Because he hadn't been able to face his own son in the knowledge that he'd been fooling around behind his wife's back?

Alessio had duly returned home to witness his father tying the knot with a woman nearly half his age.

His bitterness had been a solid lump inside him that had never shifted.

His father had never carried the burden of his beautiful wife's death. Life had moved on for him faster than a speeding bullet.

Marriage number two had ended a year and a half later in a long, acrimonious and costly divorce. It was never mentioned now. Alessio could only remember a blonde with a taste for jewellery and living the high life who had come and gone in the blink of an eye. It was just something else that was never mentioned between them.

And then the years had rolled by in ever-increasing silence until here they were now.

'It means nothing,' he drawled, vaulting upright and strolling over to where she was stirring something in a frying pan. 'Whatever it is you're concocting smells very tempting.'

Sophie stiffened as she felt him peer over her shoulder. His breath was warm against her neck and she wanted to rub the sensation away.

She had asked a simple question and yet he had changed the subject effortlessly. He was a man with a lot of *Do Not Trespass* signs posted around himself, and she wondered what lay behind those signs and then quickly reminded herself that it was none of her business.

'If you'd like to sit down…' She edged away just enough to escape his suffocating nearness, which addled her wits. 'I'll bring your food to you.'

'I'm not my father,' Alessio murmured softly. 'I'm more than capable of getting a plate for myself, and some cutlery, and dishing out my own food.'

Rattled by the tingling racing up and down her spine, Sophie stood back, leaning against the counter, and said testily, 'But can you cook the food that goes on the plate?'

Their eyes met and she reddened.

Alessio burst out laughing. For a few seconds his dark eyes roved over her burning face, before he sat down, nodding at the chair opposite him in an invitation for her to sit.

'No, I can't,' he said, and helped himself to the tomato and basil and herb sauce, dumping it over the pasta she had boiled and tossed in olive oil. 'Why deprive a decent chef of earning a living?'

'You *never* cook anything for yourself?'

Sophie sat. There was a cup of tepid tea in front of her, which she had been drinking before. She fetched them both some water and then, when he asked her whether there was any wine, poured a glass for him.

'I never drink on my own,' Alessio said.

'I don't drink on duty...'

'You're not on duty now.'

It feels like duty, Sophie thought. Or something else. Something that made her pulses leap and her cool mind suddenly begin to unravel...something that was just enough to make her nervous.

But she wasn't going to let him see that.

For one thing, she was the woman in charge of his dad and, whatever issues he and Alessio had between them, it was important that she gave the impression of being someone capable and professional. How much confidence in her abilities would Alessio have if she was flustered and tongue-tied around him?

She duly poured herself a small glass and took a sip. 'So you eat out all the time?'

'You look shocked,' he said.

'Doesn't it get a little boring?'

'I have a personal chef who cooks for me when I'm at my place.'

'You're spoilt.'

'The more I'm with you, the more you surprise me.'

'Please don't ask me where I've been hiding,' Sophie said, realising with a start that the glass of wine was nearly gone, even though she couldn't remember having any. 'I do a job. I wouldn't be here if it weren't for…for what's happening with your dad just now.'

'That was excellent.' Alessio pushed the empty plate to one side and refilled their glasses.

And seeing that simple gesture Sophie realised just how much in control he was. He started conversations when he chose to. He bypassed what he had no intention of sharing. And he was brazen when it came to prying into other people's motivations.

She had seen all the articles his father had cut out and saved over the years. Even now that online search engines had made knowledge accessible at the flick of a button, Leonard still ferreted out the most flattering and had them printed into hard copy so that he could keep them.

Every article was glowing in its praise for this guy who ruled the financial world. Every gossip column was stuffed with pictures of him somewhere, doing something important, with someone very beautiful on his arm.

He was clearly a man who played as hard as he worked.

But there was nothing that ever gave the slightest indication of what sort of man he really was on the inside.

His private thoughts and opinions on anything other than business deals were nowhere to be found.

Sophie didn't want to expend energy in thinking about the guy, because she was here to do a job and so was he. She ignored the compliment about the food and looked at him steadily until he smiled…a slow, curling smile that seemed to acknowledge every single little thought that had been running through her head.

It was disconcerting.

'Have you managed to get your accountants to look at the books?'

'They've begun,' Alessio said. 'My father's finances were decimated after his divorce, which I assume you know about, but since then it's just been the usual series of misjudged investments, an adherence to old technology and too many dinosaurs in top positions who haven't make the sort of brave decisions they should have along the way. A company run like a gentlemen's club will always end up going down the drain because in this day and age there's no room for companies like that. Have you met any of my father's business colleagues?'

'A few,' Sophie admitted.

'And what did you think of them?'

'They seemed charming, if a little old-fashioned.'

'Correct. And old-fashioned charm has its place, but not in the cut-throat world of making money.'

'Leonard isn't some young twenty-something whippersnapper,' Sophie said sharply. 'He's an elderly man with health problems.'

'Then he should have come to me the minute he discovered the mess his company was in.'

'He's in awe of you.'

Alessio stared at her with open incredulity, and then

he laughed shortly. 'I think your choice of words might be a little off target. My father has never been in awe of me or anything I have done.'

Alessio vaulted to his feet, taking his plate to the sink with him, but not doing anything with it. Certainly not washing it. Or putting it in the dishwasher.

Sophie assumed that a guy who had a personal chef on speed dial wasn't even going to know what a dishwasher was.

In the recent absence of the housekeeper, Sophie had to do all the kitchen chores herself, which she didn't begrudge, but why on earth should she do chores for Alessio, when he was perfectly capable of doing them for himself? She wasn't paid to cook or clean, but she did it because she loved Leonard and because she now knew that he couldn't afford to get anyone in to do that kind of work for him. But for Alessio…?

She carried the rest of the dishes to the counter, opened the dishwasher and nodded to it. 'You can stack,' she said, 'while I tidy the kitchen. Or else we'll come down here in the morning and it'll look as though a bomb exploded.'

'Stack the dishwasher…?'

'It's easy,' Sophie said, grudgingly amused in spite of herself and finding it hard not to soften. 'Most people don't need a degree in engineering to do it.'

'I'm being ticked off,' Alessio murmured. 'Is this because you disapprove of me not being able to cook?'

'I'm not ticking you off, and I don't care whether you can cook or not.'

The force of that dark gaze upon her was making her

skin prickle, but she remained rooted to the spot, unable to tear her eyes away, distractedly wondering how it was possible for a man to be as sinfully beautiful as this one was. There should be a law against looks like his.

'No?'

His voice was a feathery caress, and had the effect of bringing her back down to earth at speed.

'No,' she denied coolly. 'I'm asking you to help because there's no one to do the daily chores around here and it'll help me out.'

'What happened to the housekeeper?'

'In case you hadn't noticed,' Sophie told him, her voice still cool as she began wiping counters and putting things back into cupboards, all the while bringing more dishes to the sink, 'she hasn't been around for the past eight months.'

'I hadn't noticed,' Alessio said slowly, as he leant against the counter and flung the tea-towel she had handed him earlier over one shoulder. He folded his arms and stared at her with a distracted frown. 'You've been picking up the slack?'

'Who else was going to do it?'

'That hasn't been reflected in a pay rise. I would know.'

'It doesn't matter.' Sophie sighed. She thought of her own childhood. 'Believe me, doing all of this—"picking up the slack", as you call it—is something I'm accustomed to.'

Since Alessio seemed to have forgotten all about the dishwasher as he strolled towards the fridge and fetched a bottle of mineral water, Sophie loaded it herself and then made them both some coffee.

'You were going to tell me how things are going to proceed here,' she encouraged, once they were back at the kitchen table. 'It would be a good idea, so that I can plan my days accordingly.'

'Nothing will change for you,' Alessio said. His dark eyes were thoughtful. 'Except, of course, you may notice that my father's mood goes noticeably downhill while I'm around. Aside from that, you'll do what you usually do.' He looked around him. 'And you can forget about picking up the slack. I'll ensure suitable help is arranged so that you don't have to tidy up this huge pile along with all your other duties.'

'You don't have to do that.'

'Trust me when I tell you that I never do anything because I feel I have to,' Alessio said. 'It will be arranged. As for me? You won't notice I'm here.'

That was true for precisely ten hours the following day. Because Alessio, as Leonard informed her just as soon as she had prepared their breakfast and sat opposite him at the kitchen table, was off to the office, even though it was Sunday and no one would be around.

'Probably getting a head start on laying a few explosives underneath the desks,' he said, and scowled, continuing the theme which had started the second she had entered his bedroom that morning, to find him up and alert and already dressed for the day.

Leonard, now in his late seventies, still had a mane of grey hair, and although age and poor health had slowed

him down, he still possessed the demeanour of someone whose entire working life had been spent giving
orders he expected to have obeyed.

'Why do you say that?' she asked now.

'Well, you've met him! Now that he's got a bee in his
bonnet, he's not going to give up until he's sacked every
one of my CEOs! He's there right now, poring through
the files and finding out all sorts of who knows what
against who knows who!'

Sophie was adept at pouring oil on troubled waters,
and in truth she was used to Leonard's cantankerous
take on almost everything, from *'young people these
days'* to *'all this computer nonsense that's taken over
people's lives.'*

She placidly let him rant and rave until he had sub-
sided, and then they had a sensible discussion about
Alessio with only a handful of disgruntled expletives
thrown in for good measure.

Sunday was meant to be a day of relaxation. It should
have been one of her days off. But Sophie rarely took
that day to herself, because she knew that it was her employer's loneliest day—the one that seemed to stretch
into infinity for him, with no sense of purpose and
nothing to do.

It was cold and miserable today, but she drove him to
their favourite National Trust house, with its extensive
gardens, where they had a light lunch and killed some
time, he in the wheelchair he loathed, even though it
was only pulled out if he had to cover a lot of distance.

'Your son mentioned something about getting another housekeeper,' Sophie said, as she drove them back

to his own country house, the windscreen wipers not quite keeping up with the sudden freezing downpour.

'You told him that Edith had left?'

Sophie sighed and slid her eyes across to Leonard, who was glaring at her, his bushy eyebrows drawn into a black, accusatory frown.

'Don't you think he might have noticed, considering he's going to be around for longer than a handful of hours? Unless he's blind as a bat, he's going to spot that no one's appearing from the woodwork to serve the dinner and clear away the plates.'

'Hmph…'

'You're a crotchety old man, Leonard White.'

'And *you* would try the patience of saint, Miss Court, running around telling tales!' He snorted. 'But I suppose the boy *would* have noticed sooner or later,' he conceded grudgingly. 'Just one more thing to add to the list.'

'What list?'

They were back, and as she slid the car into its usual spot in the grand circular courtyard she glanced across to him to find that he was flushing, his mouth downturned.

'Nothing.'

Leonard began opening the car door and Sophie flew out so that she could unfurl the umbrella always kept on the back seat and help him out on to the drive, where he teetered and then stabilised after a couple of seconds.

'Don't you *nothing* me,' she chided as they made slow progress to the front door. 'What do you mean by that?'

'Just something else I've managed to get wrong,' he muttered, allowing himself to be helped out of his layers of waterproof clothing, which Sophie shook and neatly hung on the row of coat hooks in the cupboard by the front door.

The draught from the cold outside hung around inside the house like a miasma. It felt damp, and she hurried them into the kitchen where the Aga could be relied upon to keep the room warm.

It was later than she thought, so she made them a pot of tea and then started preparing Leonard's early dinner—toast and scrambled eggs. After that they would retire to the sitting room that adjoined his bedroom, and there they would pass an hour or so while Sophie reread some of the stuff he had previously gone through… memories filed away and now brought out and dusted down to be put on paper for the memoirs that were more a labour of love than a plan with a destination.

At the rate at which they were travelling down Leonard's memory lane, he would be two hundred before the task was completed.

She loved Leonard, and wanted to pry further into what he'd meant earlier, but when she thought of Alessio and the disturbing effect he had on her she wondered how far she should allow her curiosity to go.

The equation now wasn't just about her and Leonard. With Alessio physically in the house, it was a picture that was getting wider and broader and more encompassing, and something inside her warned against being swept away and getting too involved. Whatever simmered between father and son wasn't her business.

However, just as she was about to leave him to settle at a little after eight, he said, apropos of nothing in
particular, 'He never forgave me.'

'Alessio?' Sophie stopped and walked back to the
chair by the bedroom window, where Leonard was finishing the cup of hot chocolate she had brought up.

'The boy hates me.'

'That's not true!'

'I tried. I didn't know how. Now he's here and everything's unravelled for me. He's probably gloating
that the old idiot couldn't even run his own company
in the end! All the luxuries are gone. Can't even afford
to have someone come in to clean the place now. Up to
him to hire someone.'

'None of that's true.' Sophie was dismayed. 'And you
mustn't stress. You know what your consultant said.'

'Easier said than done, my dear.' He reached out
and squeezed her hand. 'Alessio was up at the crack of
dawn, bright-eyed and bushy-tailed and raring to tear
my company apart.'

'He isn't going to tear your company apart. He's
going to try and sort it out—and isn't that a good thing,
Leonard?' Sophie asked gently. 'If your son hated you,
wouldn't he have walked away from the responsibility?'
She was surprised to find that she meant every word as
she added, 'If there's one thing I can tell, it's this, Leonard. Alessio might be tough, but he's fair, and whatever
he does to sort the company out and ease your financial
problems it will be necessary and done with thought and
consideration for the people who might be affected.'

Leonard pursed his lips and harrumphed under his

breath, but Sophie had clearly given him something to think about, and he was lightening up and complaining about the usual things by the time she left him fifteen minutes later.

But some of the things he had said had given Sophie pause for thought, and when, an hour and a half later, Alessio strode into the kitchen, where she was nursing a mug of coffee, she had to force herself to appear natural and, more importantly, *neutral*. He was in jeans and a jumper and he was rubbing his hands together, warming himself.

'Bloody awful weather out there. You'll be pleased to hear that there's no need to cook anything for me. I've eaten.' He spared her a passing glance. 'I would have brought you back something, but I assumed you would have powered ahead without me. Tell me what you did today.'

He paced the kitchen, fetching a mug, making himself some coffee, and Sophie watched him and subliminally appreciated the graceful economy of his movements, and the way he somehow managed to own the space in which he moved.

'I didn't realise that you would be heading into the office today,' she countered, her mouth tightening as she recalled Leonard's sadness when he had so briefly confided in her earlier.

'And *I* didn't think I had to run my timetable by you on a minute-by-minute basis,' Alessio said with equal cool as he joined her at the table, sprawling back in the chair, which he somehow managed to dwarf. 'I'm here to get a job done, and how I choose to spend my time doing it isn't really in your remit. Not unless you have a list of responsibilities of which I am unaware?'

'I just thought you might have wanted to spend some time with your dad.' Sophie held her ground, without any rancour in her voice, even though again she couldn't help but marvel that a man so smart and so sexy could also be so impenetrable and so downright loathsome.

'I spent more than sufficient time with him when I popped in before I left for Harrogate,' Alessio said drily. 'I got the distinct impression that he was relieved when I was ready to go.'

'He's scared that you're going to tear his company apart.'

'He has every right to be afraid. It's a mess. I've spent the day reading through a mind-boggling array of numbers and figures and profit and loss columns, half of them filed in metal cabinets, as though the world hasn't changed since those bad old days. I've discovered lots of poor investment decisions and badly thought-out loans, and a total lack of urgency in moving in line with technological progress. Heads will need to roll, I'm afraid.'

'Will you...will you be gentle when you discuss that with him?'

'It's business, Sophie.' Alessio looked at her from under his lashes, his face revealing nothing. 'There's only so much hand-holding I can do when it comes to laying my cards on the table.'

'He's so upset already...'

Alessio frowned. 'Sometimes when you talk about my father,' he murmured, 'I almost get the impression that you're talking about someone I don't know at all.'

'He's softer than you think!'

'Really? I'm curious to see that side to him, considering it's never been in evidence in the past.'

'Are you?'

Anger twisted inside Sophie at the cool, amused indifference in Alessio's voice. Did he know his father at all? She thought of the acres of emptiness that seemed to separate them. She thought of those articles so lovingly kept, and the wobble in Leonard's voice when he'd told her that he feared his own son hated him.

Sophie had spent a lot of her formative years in situations that she should not have been in—caretaking a bewildered, lost parent and a kid sister who had needed looking after—but not once had she failed to feel overwhelming love for both of them. The very thought of Leonard despairing of his only son's affection brought a sour lump to her throat.

So devastatingly good-looking...so incredibly aloof...

'You only have one father,' she said stiffly.

'You're overstepping your job title, Miss Court.'

'I don't want anything to stress your father. It won't be good for him.'

'Then allow me to handle things my way.'

'You're so...*cold*!'

'I think you've mentioned that before. You should be careful of taking sides in a battle that's not yours.'

'I just want what's best for Leonard, and it doesn't help his health issues for him to think that you hate him...'

CHAPTER FOUR

ALESSIO STILLED.

Had he just heard what he thought he'd heard? Had anyone *ever* overstepped the boundaries as much as the woman sitting opposite him just had? For a few seconds he was quite simply so incredulous that words failed him.

'I'm sorry.' Sophie rushed hurriedly into the lengthening silence. 'I shouldn't have said that. I just…got so frustrated. I'm sorry.'

'I appreciate that you want what's best for my father…' Alessio cleared his throat and tried to wrest back some self-control. But he had taken a direct hit, and for a man who never lost his self-control, far less ever took any direct hits from anyone, he was finding himself on shaky ground.

'I do.' Sophie leant forward, every fibre of her being stretched taut, as if with a sense of urgency for him to understand her outburst.

Their eyes tangled. Alessio wondered how he could ever have described the firebrand leaning towards him as 'background'. She was about as background as a rocket taking off for Mars.

'You do?' he heard himself parrot, still dazed by what she had said. His father thought that he *hated* him? How on earth had things got to where they had?

For ten years he had had a good childhood. Of course his father had, by nature, been the more distant parent. His mother had been the laughter and the exuberance... the one who had flung things into a basket and dragged her husband from his office and dug her heels in until he laughed and agreed to take them to the beach. She had been the one who hugged and kissed and sang in the kitchen and played music, pulling her husband to his feet and twirling him round, teasing him that she would make a dancer out of him if it was the last thing she ever did.

Alessio had adored her. But he had also loved his father and looked up to him. How had that disappeared so completely over the years?

He knew how. The open water between them had grown and swelled with disagreements and nagging differences and harsh judgement calls until an ocean separated them. He had been too young to understand what had been going on with his father after his wife had died, and his lack of forgiveness for his remarrying so soon after her death had solidified into a wall of bitterness that had been cemented into place.

For the first time Alessio felt uncomfortable with the choices he had made and the road he had opted to follow.

He fidgeted and frowned, his dark gaze resting on

Sophie's expressive face. Her eyes were blazing with a mixture of determination, sincerity, and regret for what she had said in the heat of the moment. Her short blonde hair was tangled every which way, as natural as it was possible to get. Her mouth was parted.

And as his eyes drifted further down he felt a quickening inside him and a sudden heavy ache in his groin. Because out of nowhere he was imagining more than just a concerned carer. He found himself mentally undressing her, getting to the hot, passionate woman underneath.

It occurred to him that he knew nothing about her personal life. It also occurred to him, hard on the heels of that, that her personal life was none of his business.

'It's very reassuring,' he murmured now, 'to know that the person who is looking after my father is so heavily invested in his well-being.'

'Invested enough to stick up for him against her better judgement?' she asked.

'It's what brought you down to see me in London, isn't it?'

'Yes, it is. I'm very fond of Leonard.'

'Why do you qualify your sticking up for him as going against your better judgement?'

'Because...' Sophie sighed. 'It's not up to me to air anything your father should be saying to you face to face.'

'Do I intimidate you?' Alessio asked softly, his head tilted to one side.

'Of course not! Like I said... I... It's not my place...

It just sort of came out… You don't intimidate me…not at all. Why would you?'

'It's been known to happen.' Alessio shrugged. 'I have no idea why, because I am the least forbidding person I know.'

Sophie's eyebrows shot up. 'You can't know very many people, that being the case.'

Alessio smiled and relaxed. He was beginning to think that he really quite enjoyed looking at her. He also really quite enjoyed the way she didn't try to tip-toe around him or suck up to him.

Of course she was perfectly right. She had been to-tally out of order in saying what she had. But for the moment he decided that he was happy to park that par-ticular irritation to one side.

'So…' he purred. 'Moving on from the topic of my father and his financial woes just for the moment…'

'Okay…'

'Like I said, I feel immensely fortunate that you take such interest in him—but don't you have other things to occupy your time? Other things to worry about? I know we've briefly covered this, but is there no one in your life who takes issue with the amount of time you dedicate to my father?'

'What do you mean?'

'You know what I mean, Sophie. Much as I like the fact that you're devoted to my father, I wouldn't want to think that you're denying yourself the things you should be doing or feel you want to be doing.'

'I'm not.'

'I know very little about you aside from the details of your nursing qualifications.'

'Isn't that all that's relevant?'

Sophie had no idea how they had managed to get to a place where he was quizzing her about her personal life, but perhaps he had a point. Up till now she had been largely invisible, but that time was over.

The situation with Leonard meant that his son was bound to zero in on her, to take more of an interest in the role she played—especially now. Because, whether she liked it or not, he was picking up the tab for her very generous salary.

She had had no idea that Alessio was responsible for her being paid and, that being the case…yes, he might consider it his right to know more about her circumstances than he currently did.

'When my father hired you I of course made sure your qualifications were all in order, but it was up to him to decide who he wanted looking after him.'

'And what's changed now?' Sophie asked quietly.

'When you took on this role, I don't expect you ever thought it would get as complicated as it has, did you? Yes, you signed up for a time-consuming post, but was it supposed to be a full-time residential situation from the start?'

'Less than it's become recently.'

'And then there's the business of having to do all the additional duties which you've undertaken without any increase in pay to compensate. Working around the house…doing chores you weren't hired to do. I'm as-

suming that was not something you'd factored in when
you accepted the position, however generously it paid?'

'I suppose not.'

'In which case I feel it's only fair that I reassure you
straight away that if this mess is impacting in any way,
shape or form on your personal life, I will immediately
compensate you in whatever manner I deem necessary.'

Alessio knew that he was shamelessly fishing for information without asking any direct questions.

'Does that mean I will have to answer to you?' Sophie queried stiffly.

'It means that I want to make sure that you're still
happy with what you do and that all these extra responsibilities aren't being borne with hidden resentment. For
instance, the situation regarding a housekeeper should
have been brought to my attention a long time ago.'

'It was difficult...'

'I get that. You were under strict instructions to keep
me in the dark.'

Because my father thinks I hate him.

Alessio gritted his teeth, but banked down all emotion, focusing instead of the woman sitting opposite
him.

In truth, every question he'd asked was a pertinent
one, even though his original point of curiosity had been
to find out more about the woman behind the profession.

'None of that work should have been part of your
job,' he pointed out. 'But I understand that it's difficult
to disentangle one thing from another when you get involved on a personal level.'

'I've enjoyed it,' Sophie admitted. 'I haven't been secretly resentful. If I were unhappy, I would have said something. Maybe not to you, but to your father. I'm not some kind of shrinking violet who's content to put up with something she doesn't find acceptable.'

'That may be, but it still brings me right back to my original query. I don't want your absorption with all this to get in the way of your social life.' He paused and looked at her in silence for a couple of seconds. 'It's easy for that to happen. You say your friends all work odd hours... In the nursing profession I suppose that's an inevitable hazard?'

'You get used to it.'

'I assume that your social life dovetails naturally with what you do here. You don't keep traditional hours. But what about family? More importantly, what about a significant...er...*other*?'

Sophie felt the slow creep of heat and colour invade her cheeks. Was it any of his business whether there was someone in her life or not?

No!

But if she were to give him the benefit of the doubt, could he perhaps just be showing a natural concern that she might be overwhelmed by events?

She might have told him that she would never have accepted working conditions she didn't like, but working conditions that changed slowly over time fell into another category, didn't they?

Maybe, now that he was her boss in all but name, he was simply doing what any astute employer would do and making sure that a valued employee didn't have any gripes about the position they were in. The last thing he'd need would be for her to up sticks and decide to hand in her notice.

However, despite her stoic efforts to see the logic in the progression of this conversation, Sophie couldn't help but feel embarrassed to death by her singledom. Her kid sister had had more boyfriends over the years than she had!

She looked at Alessio from under her lashes and shivered. The guy was pure, unadulterated sex on legs. Everything about him was physically compelling. It wasn't simply the arrangement of his features…there was something else there that overpowered. The intelligence, the wit, the shrewdness in those fabulous dark eyes. The suggestion of a complex personality that intrigued.

She would have felt a lot more comfortable having this conversation with someone fatherly and sympathetic.

She knew that he was politely waiting for some kind of response, so eventually she shrugged and said, as nonchalantly as she could, 'There's no one in my life at the moment, so there's no need to worry that I've somehow found myself stuck with duties I hadn't banked on and having to make excuses to a guy, telling him that I'm not going to be around to cook his dinner after all. Not that I would be cooking his dinner.'

'I admit that's something of a relief,' Alessio murmured, lowering his eyes.

'And what about you?'

'Come again?'

'You? Now that you're here, and it's so important that Leonard's affairs are sorted out, is there anyone who might distract you from the task at hand?'

'Are you asking me whether there's a woman in my life?'

Alessio angled his dark head and shot her a slow smile that made her toes curl. It also made her wish that she hadn't risen to the mischievous little voice inside her that had propelled her to ask the question in the first place.

'Women can be demanding,' Sophie muttered vaguely.

'Agreed.'

'And with your father's health issues…the worry…'

'You want to make sure that I've got my mind on the task in hand and don't feel the need to rush between London and Harrogate because I have a woman waiting in the wings, demanding my undivided attention?'

'Naturally no one expects you to devote one hundred per cent of your time and energy to this…'

'I'm afraid it's a big job. Not something I can dip in and out of. I think I may be here longer than the original week I planned, having had a look at the chaos at the company.'

'But how on earth are you going to be able to do that?'

The dynamic in the house had changed with Alessio's arrival, and Sophie was privately alarmed at the prospect of him being around indefinitely. How on earth was her nervous system going to stand it? He did things to her she didn't like. He made her aware of her sexuality, which was something she had put on the back burner to be brought out at some later date.

A lifetime of inherited caution when it came to the opposite sex had ended up being an enemy of adventure when it came to putting herself out there...experimenting with sex and the messy business of relationships. It had been easier to step back completely, to hand herself over to making money so that she could sort out the financial obligations of her family. And then all the stuff with Leonard had made it impossible for her to do anything other than focus on her job.

None of which had prepared her for the effect Alessio was having on her. It was as though his presence in the house and the vitality he radiated in his aggressive masculinity had awakened something in her she had hardly been aware existed.

'The worldwide web,' Alessio said succinctly. 'You'd be surprised how much can be done remotely. The problem here is that it's a hands-on situation. It involves interviewing people and asking questions, identifying the dead wood and extracting it. You can't do any of that from a distance on a computer. But, to get back to your original question, no, there's no one waiting in the wings in London, tapping her watch and asking me when I'll be home...'

'Of course you could always bring your partner here to stay,' Sophie mumbled indistinctly.

'I wouldn't have dreamt of doing that even if I had been dating someone.'

'Why not? It's an enormous house. You could have had your own separate quarters.'

Curiosity dug its claws into her. She had seen pictures of Alessio and the revolving door of gorgeous blondes he dated, and she wondered how it was that none of them ever stayed the course. Did he work so hard that he didn't give any thought to settling down?

'I don't share my space with anyone,' Alessio said abruptly, and Sophie's eyes widened.

'Okay,' she said hurriedly.

'Do you?'

'I beg your pardon?'

'Share your space…?'

Alessio glanced around him just as she had done, putting the same question to her with a single inquisitive look that was tinged with wicked amusement.

'I'm sure my father wouldn't have a problem with you bringing your partner here to live in with you, as long as it didn't distract you from your duties. Or has there been no partner to distract you for the past couple of years?' He grinned and waved his hand in a dismissive manner. 'I sense you're about to make an objection to that line of questioning, so before you can do that I withdraw the question.' He looked at her seriously. 'But we're going to be in one another's company, so perhaps we can have some kind of informal arrangement worked out?'

'Good idea.'

'Tell me how you spend your day and what sort of time my father retires to bed.' He glanced at his watch. 'Very early, you've told me. Would that be every night?'

'Recently, yes. In the past, less so.'

'His health problems leave him tired?'

'And everything that's been on his mind as well,' Sophie said pensively, sliding her eyes away from Alessio's mesmeric stare, which made it easier for her to collate her thoughts. 'It can be exhausting when your brain is churning over things, worrying away at problems. It can keep you up at night, and then insomnia becomes a habit that's difficult to shake.'

'Is that a fact...?' Alessio said softly.

Sophie blinked and reddened.

'Are you speaking from experience?' Alessio asked. Their eyes met.

Sophie felt the rebuff dry up in her throat, because the eyes that collided with hers were oddly encouraging. How was that possible? How could she disapprove of someone, feel unsettled by them, and yet be drawn to confide, which was how she felt now?

Was it because he was a stranger? Because confidences were more easily shared with someone you didn't personally know?

Or was it just part of his enormous magnetism that he fascinated, attracted and repelled in equal measure...?

Her mouth was dry and her breathing shallow as she was pinned into silence by his eyes.

'Well? Tell me...'

'I... I've had my fair share of problems,' Sophie heard herself admit shakily. 'My father died when I was young, and my mother fell apart. I have a kid sister... Adelaide. And for a little while—well, quite a long while, as it happens—I had to look after both of them because my mum couldn't cope. I had to deal with…a lot. Social workers…the council… I grew up fast, and it was a very anxious time, so, yes, I know what it's like to lose sleep. And once you've lost it, it's very difficult to find it again.'

She offered a watery, apologetic smile, but Alessio didn't smile back. His dark eyes were serious and concerned.

'You took this job because it paid so well, didn't you?'

'What makes you say that?'

'Nursing in a hospital is a busy job. You're surrounded by people and there's a lot going on. That's a far cry from what you have here.'

'I love working for your father.'

'I'm not disputing that, but I'm guessing the money played a part. If life has been tough for you, perhaps, along with having to deal with a parent who couldn't cope, you've also had to deal with financial problems that kept you awake at night?'

Sophie shrugged and then nodded.

The distance between them seemed to have closed. Had he dragged his chair closer to hers? Had she somehow edged hers closer to his? Their knees were almost touching. When she glanced down she could see the strain of his jeans, pulled taut over his muscular thighs.

This was where a lack of experience got a girl. One minute she had been happily plodding along, content in her own inertia, and then just like that along came Alessio and everything was suddenly tossed into the air.

Her head was suddenly filled with should-haves, and she felt tears prick the back of her eyes.

She was horrified. She never cried. She wasn't a crier—because what was the point of crying over stuff that couldn't be changed? And the past could never be changed.

She stood up and shambled towards the sink with her mug. She began washing it, just for something to do. With her back to him, she was unaware of him behind her until she felt his hands on her shoulders, drawing her round to look at him.

'I've upset you,' he said roughly.

'No!'

'If I had had any idea of what was going on I would have been here in a hurry, whether my father wanted it or not.'

'Of course.'

'You're not being paid to carry someone else's stress on your shoulders. Even if it's something you've been accustomed to doing. How is your mother now? Your sister? Time must have moved on for all of you. But is there anything I can do to help financially?'

The utter kindness of his gesture was too much.

Overwhelmed and wrong-footed by the very fact that she had opened up to someone about her past, Sophie felt one treacherous tear slip down her cheek. Mortified, she tried to shake her head free, but his grip tightened.

'You can cry,' he said gruffly.

She shot him a wobbly smile. 'Is that an order from my new boss?'

'I'm not your new boss.'

'You...you've just said...'

'You will always only ever answer to my father. And...off the record...there's no need for the old man to think that anything's changed on that front.'

Sophie nodded jerkily and drew in a deep breath to steady her nerves.

'Your mother and sister?' Alessio went back to what he had asked her before they were side-tracked. 'Anything I can do?'

'Thank you, but everything is under control. Thanks to the pay I've been receiving here,' Sophie admitted, letting another confidence slip through the net. 'My mother is settled in a little place by the coast, where she's made some friends and got a life for herself. After everything was sorted and the bills and debts paid I managed to get the mortgage there right down. And my sister... I can help her too. She's an aspiring actress.'

'An actress and a nurse?' Alessio mused. 'I'm getting the picture.'

Sophie brushed the tear from her cheek, and this time her smile was rueful but genuine. She stepped back, and was relieved when he released her and also stepped back. But the atmosphere had shifted, and when their eyes met there was a charge in the air that hadn't been there before. It slithered, electric and dangerous, barely visible but *there*. She knew that her heart had picked up pace and she couldn't tear her eyes away from his dark, intent stare.

Alessio couldn't remember the last time any woman had had this effect on him. In truth, he had encouraged confidences in a way he was not accustomed to doing. He was a man who didn't rush into caveman protective mode at the sight of tears. In fact a crying woman had the effect of making his teeth snap together with impatience, and it wasn't because he was hard-hearted. It was because female tears were usually, in his experience, a prelude to pleading for a relationship Alessio had always made sure to warn against from the beginning.

He could understand how Sophie had learned life lessons from what she had described of her childhood and adolescence.

He had learned his own.

The past was a country Alessio tried his best not to revisit. What was the point? But being here, back in the house in which he had grown up, which he was now tasked to save, was bringing back memories of the past.

Memories of happier times before his mother had died.

Times before the shutters had come down, separating him from his father with a wall that had ended up too solid to climb.

And now memories of his stepmother, a greedy gold-digger who had married his father with clearly only one thing in mind and that was his money.

Young as he had been at the time, he had disliked the woman instinctively, and what had followed—the acrimonious divorce and the long-winded proceedings during which she had done her utmost to get hold of whatever assets she could—had taught a youthful Alessio that when it came to the opposite sex it paid to be careful. If you took your eye off the ball you were always going to be the one who paid the price.

His father's divorce had taken over six years to reach a conclusion, and during that time those walls between them had grown higher and more impregnable.

He frowned now, a little thrown by the way the past was making itself felt. He raked his fingers through his hair and sought to get the conversation back on track, because just for a second he'd wanted to step back towards the woman in front of him, whose eyes were still glistening with unshed tears.

He gritted his teeth and shifted, but his feet refused to walk away.

'What picture is that?' she asked.

Alessio sensed her desire to break the silence. He breathed in deep. 'You the older, sensible one, allowing your kid sister to live the life you denied yourself?'

'Maybe...'

'It must have been tough.'

'I managed.'

'Everyone can *manage*,' Alessio mused, considering how he had done the same, and probably at a very similar age. 'But it's good to go beyond that.'

His hands itched to touch her. He clenched his fists. But then he did what he'd sworn not to do and reached to brush the side of her face with his fingers.

It was a light, barely-there touch.

Sophie froze. She couldn't breathe, couldn't move, could barely get her brain to work at all.

He'd touched her.

And the touch hadn't been brotherly and empathetic. The touch had carried the pulsing feel of something sexual...something else.

Or was that all in her fevered imagination?

She wanted to close her eyes and pull him closer.

She wanted his mouth to go where his fingers still were, stroking her cheek.

The klaxon bells warning of danger were muted as she took a trembling step towards him, and when she looked at him, lips parted, her whole body alive with sudden craving, she could see the very same thing mirrored in his dark eyes.

Desire...

She heard her own soft exhalation and felt her eyelids flutter on a gasp as his fingers traced the contours of her mouth, one finger dipping inside. She sucked on that finger, drawing it in, pulling them closer.

His kiss was shattering.

She had expected it, had wanted it, had *feared* it.

His mouth crushed hers even as he drew her against his hard, muscular body. His tongue was a sweet invasion and turned her world upside down.

Never, ever had Sophie experienced anything like this. She'd never even imagined it possible to be so overwhelmed by sheer physical need for someone.

She wound her hands around his neck, stretching up, her breasts sensitive and tingling as they rasped against the cotton of her bra.

It was a moment of complete surrender.

But then common sense kicked in, swiftly followed by horror. Had she felt something similar in him? She imagined she had as she pulled away, devastated by what had just happened.

She looked at him, a hand over her mouth. 'I...'

'Me too.' Alessio stepped back, his fabulous dark eyes shuttered. 'This never happened.' One more step back. 'A moment in time. Nothing more. Tomorrow my work begins in earnest, and you will see next to nothing of me.'

'Good,' Sophie said curtly.

She looked away, down to her trembling fingers, which she curled into a steady fist.

His 'moment in time' had been a shattering awakening for her. He was more than dangerous, so seeing nothing of him while he was here was what she needed. And wanted.

She turned her back on him, waited, and when she eventually turned around the kitchen was empty.

CHAPTER FIVE

SOPHIE APPROACHED THE dining room with apprehension. It had been two days since she had laid eyes on Alessio, and during that time there had not been a single minute when he hadn't been in her head.

That kiss...that moment in time...to be forgotten...

It was seared into her consciousness with the red-hot intensity of a branding iron. Yes, of course it would never happen again, but neither, for her, would it ever be forgotten.

For him...yes, it *would* be forgotten—had probably been forgotten already. Because he was a man of the world to whom a kiss was just a kiss, and it hadn't even been a kiss with a woman he was really attracted to. It had been a kiss born of sudden shared confidences and a moment during which the walls between them had been temporarily dislodged.

A matter of seconds...

Fundamentally, nothing had changed. He was still the sort of man of whom she disapproved, from the way he treated his own father to his casual approach to relationships with women. For all his sharp intelligence and complex light and shade personality, he was still not the sort of upfront, honest, straightforward kind of man she had always imagined herself eventually going for.

She had no plans ever to be knocked for six, made vulnerable. Because she couldn't cope with the love of her life being taken from her, either through death or divorce. She would never be helpless. The kind of man who could give her what she wanted in life would be someone who appealed intellectually, who was kind, and allowed her space, who was thoughtful and undemanding…someone calming, with whom she would feel comfortable. No highs or lows.

Alessio was a raging volcano, and she had no time for those. However powerful the pull to gaze into the seething red-hot lava.

And for him?

Well, how many times had he mocked her for being 'background'? What did that imply? It implied that he found her dull and unexciting…the sort of girl who was always be the wallflower, standing at the back of the room, watching everyone else have fun, waiting for her turn to arrive.

Not that far from the truth, as it happened.

She knew the sort of women Alessio liked and dated. Outgoing, sexy little blondes who paraded their assets and were as 'background' as a firework display on New Year's Eve.

And yet for all her common-sense reasoning he still remained embedded in her head like a burr.

And now, as she hesitated in front of the dining room door, she could feel her heart accelerate.

So much had been accomplished in the space of a couple of days.

A housekeeper had been hired. Leonard had announced that only the morning before.

'Just when I had become perfectly accustomed to the two of us in the house, what does the boy go and do? Another housekeeper! She'll have to work around me, my girl, that's for sure!'

Sophie had been quietly relieved, and she knew that Leonard had been as well. He was fastidious, and over the months had insisted on many of the rooms being closed so that they wouldn't become cluttered, wouldn't need cleaning. He'd used to entertain his friends in the grand sitting room, with dinner served by Edith in the dining room, but things had become a lot more informal. Gatherings had been smaller, and held in the kitchen, where Sophie had been only too happy to tease his elderly friends and join them as they ate at the kitchen table.

The company overhaul had also begun. This too she'd learnt from Leonard, who had grudgingly admitted that Alessio was not playing the tough taskmaster and flinging all his CEOs out of their offices by the seat of their trousers.

'He was never going to do that,' Sophie had soothed, smiling. 'You should know that, of all people. You've got all those cuttings and clippings stashed in folders. You admire him. You would never admire someone cruel enough to get rid of your friends and colleagues at the company.'

'The boy's ruthless.'

But Sophie had detected a thread of admiration in Leonard's voice. Yes, Alessio was ruthless, because she guessed that was what you had to be to climb the greasy pole to success, but ruthless didn't necessarily mean cruel or unfair, and Alessio was neither.

She'd shrugged and then reddened when Leonard had looked at her with narrowed, thoughtful eyes. 'Plays the field as well,' he had said slyly, and Sophie had gone a deeper shade of beetroot.

'So it would seem,' she'd murmured.

'Women fall for him. Has his mother's striking looks, that boy. Isabella was a beauty. Wouldn't want you to get swept away, my girl.'

'That would never happen.'

'He's going to be here for a couple of weeks, he says...'

'I'm immune to men like your son, Leonard.'

She had vigorously begun fluffing cushions on the sofa where he'd been relaxing in the small sitting room that adjoined his bedroom.

'Good, because you're my gentle little thing, Sophie. Wouldn't want to see you hurt by that son of mine.'

Sophie had brushed that off with a quip about him making her sound about as assertive as a bowl of jelly, but she had been embarrassed, and she was embarrassed now as she pushed open the dining room door and paused for a few seconds to take in the scene.

The dining room table was a highly polished affair that could comfortably seat twelve. At one end sat Alessio, at the other was Leonard, and roughly in the middle a setting had been laid for her.

Alessio's computer was on the table next to him, and next to Leonard. was a stack of paperwork, and both men were paying a lot more attention to the files and the computer than they were paying to one another.

'I'm sorry, but I think I'll have my dinner in the kitchen,' Sophie said with impatient frustration, at which point both men looked at her with such identical frowns that it would have been funny if it had been a different situation.

'This is ridiculous,' she burst out.

'What is, my dear?' Leonard looked startled as he half rose to his feet, frown deepening.

'This…! Sitting around this table as though we're all complete strangers! We're going to have to shout to one another to be heard!'

'Bit of an exaggeration, don't you think?' This cool rejoinder came from Alessio, who was looking at her with one eyebrow raised.

'No, I do *not*!' She glared at Alessio. If this was his way of not stressing his father out, then heaven help them all if he decided that he wasn't going to play ball with the doctor's orders.

She stormed out of the room and returned two seconds later with an amused housekeeper, who tried hard not to grin as she hastily rearranged the seating so that the three of them were huddled up close at one end of the table.

Sophie had no idea where that act of bravado had come from. Perhaps the tension of uninvited feelings had been swirling dangerously inside her and had come to a head at the sight of the man who had put them there by kissing her. The man who had ripped aside her careful self-control and tempted her into doing something that couldn't have been a bigger mistake.

Or maybe Leonard's words of warning had struck home, had made her see how ridiculous the situation was, how absolutely crazy it was that she could be attracted to Alessio. And seeing him here, lounging in all his elegant, sophisticated, *sexy* glory, had rammed home the idiocy of her wayward attraction.

At any rate, with some of the formality removed, computer closed and paperwork shoved to one side, the meal which had been prepared by Sarah, a young student who had taken up the job of housekeeper so that she could study without the pressure of a student loan hanging over her head, was enjoyed.

They talked about food.

It was not a contentious issue. Although Leonard complained about his restrictive diet, and with some attempt at light-hearted banter Alessio wondered aloud how she, Sophie, coped with him.

'She says you're a pussycat,' Alessio drawled, as their plates were removed.

Their eyes met, Sophie's tangling with Alessio's, and for a few taut seconds she felt as though the ground had been whooshed away from under her feet. All she could taste in her mouth was *him*…the wetness of his tongue probing, demanding, questing.

Her voice was croaky when, at last, she broke the silence with a suitably non-committal reply and a jerky laugh.

She could feel Leonard's sharp eyes on her and she knew she was blushing.

'We do get along,' Leonard murmured, with just a hint of smugness. 'She reads me like a book.'

'In that case,' Alessio returned, his voice lazy but laden with silky intent, 'perhaps your soulmate might care to let me know how things will pan out now that I've had a good look around this house. It's in need of a great deal of work.'

'Not going to happen is what she would say! House is perfectly fine as it is!'

'There are cracks in places cracks shouldn't be, and a suspicion of damp in several of the rooms.'

'Not going to happen!' Leonard banged his cutlery on the table and glared.

'I came here to sort things out,' Alessio gritted in a driven undertone.

'That does not include ripping my house apart!'

'I won't be ripping it apart. You were worried that I was going to storm into your offices and chuck everyone out on their ears! Have I done that?'

'If I had known you would start a campaign of home improvement I would never have allowed you to…to… help out.'

'You had no choice, Dad.'

Sophie was fascinated by this back and forth—two powerful personalities at war. She could see both sides, but was quietly impressed that Alessio was going beyond what had been put on the table originally to help out with the business.

'Sorting out the company finances isn't something I begrudge doing,' Alessio muttered. 'And getting this

house back on its feet isn't something I'm going to begrudge doing either.'

'You don't understand, son.'

'What don't I understand?'

'I don't want... Your mother...'

He flung his napkin to the table and staggered up,
and Sophie raced to his side, stricken.

'Your mother...she's here with me. I don't want that
to change. I don't want anything about this house to
change. Her soul is here and I don't want it to go away.'

Leonard waved his hands about, and just like that
Alessio was standing opposite her.

Their eyes met and there was an urgent request in
his as he said, in a low voice over his father's head, 'I'll
take it from here.'

Leonard had slumped, a diminished figure, his weakness evident now that the bluster had been blown aside.

'Of course,' Sophie said without hesitation.

'But wait here for me. Apologise to Sarah and tell her
that dessert will have to wait until tomorrow.'

'Yes, of course.'

She felt Leonard fumble with her hand, and she
squeezed his fingers in return and watched as Alessio
walked, supporting him, out of the dining room.

This was what it must feel like to be in the eye of a
storm, Sophie thought, sinking into her chair.

She was barely aware of Sarah entering, or even
of telling her that there would be no need for dessert
and that she could head home. Her mind was all over
the place.

'Is everything okay?' asked Sarah. 'I don't mind staying on…'

Sophie looked at the tiny, earnest young girl and smiled. 'Make sure you get a cab back to your parents, Sarah, and I'll see you in the morning.'

It was not yet seven-thirty. Should she remain seated at the dining table? Sophie had no idea how long Alessio would be, and she could barely keep still because of her anxieties.

Her head all over the place, she went into the kitchen and began clearing away the dishes. She took her time as the minutes ticked past, stretching into an hour… longer.

The routine of the kitchen…the cleaning of the counters and putting things away in their proper places…was soothing, and she was just beginning to relax when she was aware of Alessio in the kitchen with her.

When had he come in?

She didn't know.

She swung round to find him lounging in the doorway, his face paler than usual, fingers hooked over the waistband of his jeans.

In the middle of stacking the dishwasher, Sophie stopped and stared at him with concern. 'How is he?'

'Sit. I'll make us some coffee. Has Sarah gone home?'

Sophie nodded and sidled to one of the chairs, and watched as Alessio strolled into the kitchen, his movements less graceful than usual. He made coffee. Instant. Two mugs. His black, hers white with no sugar.

He dragged over a chair so that he was sitting close enough for her to reach out and touch him.

'Well?'

'I've been a long time...'

'I didn't expect you to be back downstairs in five minutes. Leonard was very upset. He would have needed calming. I should have gone...'

'Not your responsibility. What happened was my fault entirely. I never meant to stress my father out... and I'm ashamed that I did. It was unforgivable—as I made clear to him when I took him upstairs.' Alessio looked at her in brooding silence for a few seconds. 'I feel like you're caught in the middle of something you never realised you'd signed up to...'

'What does that mean?'

'I think you know perfectly well what I'm talking about.' Alessio smiled wryly, but his dark eyes remained sharp and deadly serious. 'My father and I have not had the easiest of relationships over the years.' He paused. 'I've already mentioned that. But what you just sat through...'

Sharing confidences? It was a game Alessio didn't play. He had learnt to share only what was necessary. He had never spoken about his fractured relationship with his father to anyone. Even as a young boy, dispatched to boarding school with the memory of his mother's death still fresh in his head, he had learnt how to carry the burden of his misery alone. Let down by his father, he had toughened up and learnt not to trust anyone.

When his father had remarried, Alessio's emotional

independence had become total. Now, however, he had to concede that the woman sitting opposite him with the big brown eyes and the cropped blonde hair had a right to know something of the situation into which she had unwittingly been brought.

His father depended on her far more than Alessio had ever suspected—but then there seemed to be an awful lot about his father he knew nothing about. The years had drifted by, and every passing year had placed another row of bricks in the wall separating them.

'You mentioned that you two have had your differences over the years,' Sophie said, then added quickly, 'But there's no need for you to…er…talk about anything you don't want to talk about.'

'That's very generous of you, but considering you've had something against me ever since you first started working for my father—'

'That's not true. Of course I haven't had anything against you.'

'No? Maybe not all the time. When I kissed you, you *definitely* didn't have anything against me. Aside, that is, from your body, which seemed very keen to get a bit more friendly.'

'You said that was never going to be mentioned again!'

'So I did,' Alessio murmured.

He shifted, irritated with himself for having been so easily and swiftly diverted from the matter of hand. This was a serious talk, and yet the nearness of her, that slightly floral smell that tantalised him, the silky smoothness of her skin and the calm intelligence in her eyes…

It was all messing with his head, and to someone who never allowed *anything* to mess with his head, it was frustrating.

Yet, staring at her, he just couldn't resist harking back to that kiss…that five-second, utterly earth-moving kiss that had knocked him for six.

He wanted to see her reaction to that kiss again.

He wanted to have another glimpse behind that smooth, serene mask.

He felt a soaring sense of triumph at the delicate colour that crept into her cheeks, and at the way her eyes suddenly scrupulously avoided his.

Alessio was bewildered by his own reactions.

He had not led a celibate life. He enjoyed women and women enjoyed him. It was a mutually rewarding experience. And the women he had enjoyed over the years had ranged from catwalk beautiful to downright voluptuously sexy.

He had never gone for subtle—always associating that with a woman who'd want more than he would ever be prepared to give. He liked everything upfront, all cards on the table, no mysteries to be explored.

Was he so now arrogant that the pull of the novel and the unexplored was too great to resist?

Sophie Court worked for his father, and she was the last woman on the planet in whom he should be interested.

She was a serious woman who took things seriously, and from what she had told him about herself he suspected that she would only contemplate a relationship if it came with signposts to all sorts of destinations he had no interest in exploring.

In fact, wasn't that partly why she disapproved of him? He was certain of it.

Yet it was so tempting to continue this taboo conversation, he thought. So tempting to court that delicate blushing colour again...to savour her reaction to him.

Serious she might be—but, heck, she was woman enough to have enjoyed a taste of the frivolous.

He liked that.

But he didn't like it enough to play with fire, he told himself shakily.

'My father remarried very soon after my mother died.' Alessio brought himself back down to earth in the most ruthless fashion possible, by launching into a difficult, touchy-feely conversation of the kind he fundamentally loathed and never did.

'Clarissa?' Sophie said.

'You know about her? Of course you do. You know more about my father than I do.'

'We spend a lot of time together.'

'What has he said about her?'

'Does it matter? I shouldn't have let slip that I knew who you were talking about.'

'Why? For the first time, just now, my father and I had something of a conversation that wasn't entirely rooted in the superficial. One thing I found out was just how much he depends on you—and not just for nursing care. Maybe you came here with that as your original intention, but it's clear that your relationship has progressed far beyond that. As he confided to me, you're more of a daughter to him than a nurse.'

'He said that?'

'Yes, he did.' Alessio paused. Then, 'In my absence, I have to concede that his affections have been distributed elsewhere.' He suddenly sat back and flung wide his arms. 'I should have kept my eye on the ball—but there you go. No point dwelling on things that could have been done. Fact is, he's scared of dying, and I bitterly regret stressing him out earlier. But I've managed to at least reassure him on what's happening within the company.'

'He loves you.'

'Let's not go there.'

'I just don't want you to think that because Leonard cares about me somehow you've been pushed to one side.'

'The thought never crossed my mind. And if it had it certainly wouldn't cause me any kind of existential angst. Things are as they are.' He paused and relaxed into the chair, looking at her carefully, his dark head tilted to one side. 'I never forgave my father for remarrying so soon after my mother died,' Alessio said bluntly.

'No… It must have been tough on you.'

'But it would seem that there was a story that had more to it than whatever scenario had been evolving in my head at the time. I was a kid. My father had ceased all lines of communication and I was left at the mercy of my youthful imagination. Clarissa, as he's finally confessed, was just someone he clutched at to try and cope with his grief.'

* * *

'It happens…' Sophie murmured gently.

But when she thought about a young, confused Alessio, away from his father, wordlessly thinking the worst and shutting down emotionally because of that, her heart constricted.

She had been guilty of seeing only one side of the story—Leonard's side. She had seen the clippings and the articles, and because she had become so fond of him had been angry at his son for being so cold and dismissive. She had been sure the guy who had seldom shown up was the one at fault.

She was reminded of what he had said to her a while back—that there were always two sides to every story.

'I came here,' Alessio continued heavily, 'to sort out my father's business.'

'And the fact that that's going well will really help Leonard's state of mind,' she told him. 'He might be grumpy, but I know he's relieved that things have been taken out of his hands.'

Their conversation was factual enough now, but there was a thrilling undertow that made Sophie's pulses race. Every nerve in her body was stretched taut and she found it difficult to wrest her eyes away from his.

Confiding didn't come easy to Alessio. She knew that, the situation being what it was, he probably felt cornered into saying more to her than he wanted to. Heck, he had barely noticed her existence for the past couple of years! She could have been a pot plant languishing in the corner of a room for all the attention he had paid her!

But things had changed. Did he think that he had to include her because she had become an important part of his father's life? Or had that kiss shifted the ground underneath them?

It certainly had for her, whether she wanted to admit it or not.

He'd told her that it had been nothing but a blip, a moment to be forgotten, and yet when he had referred to it moments earlier she had felt the feathery brush of lust graze her skin all over again.

She reeled at her treacherous body, which demanded to know what it might feel like to savour that touch of his again, to feel his cool lips on hers. To feel more than that.

'How much…um…longer do you see yourself being here…?' Sophie asked, internally squirming at her private thoughts.

Alessio let that question nestle into the silence as he looked at her thoughtfully. In the space of just a little over an hour—which was how long he had been upstairs with his father—things had changed.

His father had opened up. A crack. Alessio had thought himself beyond having his ideas changed. He had spent a lifetime honing them, after all. But when Leonard had gruffly told him why he had rushed headlong into that catastrophic second marriage he had hung his head and roughly brushed away tears Alessio had never thought he'd witness in a million years…

New possibilities had started to emerge from his cast-iron beliefs.

'Longer than I anticipated,' he said now. 'I hadn't taken into account how fragile my father is. I've always thought of him as...not just tough as nails, but wily with it. Seems in my absence things have changed. I don't want to jeopardise his recovery, and there's plenty more on the way that might push things in that direction.'

'What do you mean?' Sophie asked in alarm.

'I told you I've looked around this house...' Alessio glanced around him briefly. 'I've broached this subject in the past but been knocked back. Now, however, seems a good enough time to broach it again. If the company is being overhauled, then why not do the house?'

'You're really going to overhaul the house? I know you said that at the table...but Leonard seems so against it...'

'Like I said earlier, it needs doing. I've spoken to my father now, told him all the problems he'll be storing up if he puts off having essential work done, and I think he's come round to the idea. Mostly because he doesn't have a choice.'

'He seemed very adamant that that wasn't what he wanted...'

'Well, as you've witnessed, he seems to think that if the bricks and mortar gets bashed about a little, then it's somehow disrespectful to the memories stored inside them. But I've managed to persuade him that the memories are inside *him*. The house is just a house.'

'It's not that easy.'

Sophie remembered how hard it had been for her mother to leave the house she had shared with her husband for so many years. Even though by then she had ploughed her way through her heartache and misery, the final act of saying goodbye to the four walls of that house had still represented a huge change and a frightening one.

Leonard wouldn't be leaving his house, but he would face seeing it knocked about and brought up to date, perhaps remodelled in places. Because Alessio was right—there were structural issues in some of the rooms that would certainly need looking at.

She knew that life had been tough for Leonard in the past few years. He had been forced to walk away from running his company and then he'd had to deal with ill health—which had, in turn, affected his mental health.

'He needed someone to lean on,' she couldn't resist saying, her voice cool. 'He needed *you* to be here.'

'That wasn't what he wanted at the time,' Alessio grated.

'So when is this work going to begin? What is it going to entail?'

'It's going to entail my father moving out for possibly a couple of weeks. There will be workmen in and out of all the rooms, and the dust and noise will be too much for him to endure.'

'And he's *agreed* to this?'

'I've told him that there's not much choice. It's either get it done or watch the place slowly fall apart, until it becomes too difficult to patch it up the way he would like it to be. I'll be keeping as much intact as possible. But there are a lot of historic features that need renovating badly—and quickly. The stained-glass windows on the landing are about to come crashing down because they need urgent re-leading.'

'I'm not following you. Where is he going to move to? London? Leonard has always told me how much he hates London.'

'Not that he's actually been there more than a handful of times,' Alessio returned drily. 'But no. London isn't what I have in mind.'

'Then where?'

'I have a place at Lake Garda in Northern Italy. It's close enough to get there on my private jet in a matter of hours, so the trip shouldn't be too taxing for him.'

'Oh, right… Okay…'

'If we plan on leaving in roughly a week's time, it will give me sufficient time to get the ball rolling with my father's company, so that I can instal some of my own people to tie up the loose ends. I'll also have enough time for my PA to source the best crew available to get the job done here, and of course, there will have to be some time spent packing away anything valuable that needs to be protected. I suggest several of the more robust rooms in the West Wing would be suitable for that.'

'Wait, hang on just a minute… *We*…?'

'You don't think that my father is going to be able to travel without you, do you? I'm assuming you have a passport that's up to date?'

'Yes, but—'

'There aren't really a whole lot of *buts* about it,' Alessio interrupted, before any of her objections could be raised. 'If I'm honest, part of my father's agreement to this—aside from accepting the inevitability of having the house renovated—is based on the assumption that you will provide the continuity of care he needs by being there with him.'

He paused and delivered her a searching look that brought a flame of bright colour to her cheeks.

'Aside from which, what obligations do you have that might be a spoke in the wheel? Naturally, you will be richly compensated for the inconvenience, but it's hardly as though you have compelling personal duties that require your presence here, is it?'

CHAPTER SIX

ALESSIO'S PRIVATE JET landed four days later at a small airport near Milan. During those four days, Sophie's life had accelerated at supersonic speed.

Alessio had moved three of his top people into Leonard's offices in Harrogate, and taken himself back to London so that he could co-ordinate a crew to—as he had told both Sophie and Leonard before he disappeared—*'throw everything at the estate with no expense spared'*.

He had also arranged for a team of highly experienced house-movers to transfer whatever needed taking from one part of the house to another.

'Leave all the big items,' he had instructed. 'They'll be covered over and protected and it'll be a waste of time to shift them. Just move what you deem necessary.'

Predictably, Leonard had grumbled.

'One minute the boy's barely speaking to me,' he had complained on the evening before the movers had been due to arrive, 'and the next he's giving orders as though he's the master of the house!'

'You've been talking together,' Sophie had pointed

out. 'He took you out for lunch before he left for London and you seemed to have a good time.'

'Of course I'm going to be suitably polite when someone invites me somewhere,' he had huffed. 'Such a thing as good manners, my girl! Not that you'd think they still existed when you look around you nowadays!'

She had done a rapid tour of the house, pushing Leonard in the wheelchair to spare him walking from one room to another, and in the end only very personal possessions had been moved. His computer, his memoirs, and the entire collection of newspaper clippings he had collected over the years, along with photo albums and other mementoes.

She had managed to persuade him that large-scale breakages weren't going to happen. 'These people are experienced,' she had told him, gently but firmly, 'and they'll have Alessio to answer to if they make any mistakes.'

'I suppose the boy does have his head screwed on when it comes to taking charge,' Leonard had said with grudging admiration. 'Gets that from me—not that you'd know it, seeing me in this state now. Isabella, his mother...well, that was a different matter. Depended on me for just about every decision! Could never lose patience with her, though—not with that smile of hers. Could move mountains, that smile.'

Sarah had been asked to check at the end of each day to see what had been done and to make sure that Alessio's rules of tidiness were being strictly obeyed.

Alessio had summoned her before he left, and Sophie had felt sorry for the poor kid, who was so clearly in awe of Alessio that she could barely string a sentence together.

But he had been kind, and patient, and had politely overlooked her beetroot-red face and her self-conscious stammering and gently told her to get in touch with his PA. Her pay would be reviewed and increased accordingly, because of the extra responsibility of keeping an eye on the builders.

'Are they trustworthy? Will they need supervision?' Sophie had asked in alarm, when Sarah had left the room.

At a little after four in the afternoon, Leonard had been in his sitting room, relaxing, and she had been alone with Alessio, who had wanted to fill her in on arrangements before he returned briefly to London.

They'd been on opposite sofas in one of the sitting rooms. Between them on a small, old-fashioned wooden table had been a pot of tea and some biscuits Sarah had baked earlier.

'Utterly trustworthy and they won't need supervision.'

'But...'

'Sarah's nineteen, a hard worker, and she wants to save money. But I think she would be embarrassed if I were to offer to pay her while we're away for doing nothing. This way, she's doing something, and she'll get compensated for the fact that she's going to have to come here at six every evening and spend an hour or so doing the rounds.'

'That's very...thoughtful,' Sophie had conceded.

And then she had reddened when he had looked at

her in silence for a few seconds before saying, with cool amusement, 'I occasionally can be...despite the reputation that seems to have preceded me.'

She had been relieved when he had left for London, and had thrown herself into getting everything in order before they left.

And now here they were.

Travelling on Alessio's private jet had taken Sophie into the realms of ridiculous wealth. Sleek and black, it had waited for them on the tarmac of the airfield like a giant bird of prey, throwing all the other small little hoppers into pitiful shade. People had stared as they had been ushered inside, and she had sucked in her breath and paused just for a moment as she'd glanced around at an interior of cream and beige and dove-grey and walnut.

Breathtaking wealth bred breathtaking respect, and during the flight she and Leonard had been deferred to like royalty.

Leonard had promptly begun dozing, the second they were in the air, but Sophie had been too awestruck to do anything but guiltily revel in the novelty of being flown in spectacular style.

Now, as she disembarked from the obscenely lavish private jet, nerves that had been in abeyance returned with force.

'He told me about this place.' Leonard appeared next to her and they began to descend the metal stairs that had been put in place as soon as the jet had come to a stop. 'He's only had it for a few years. Wish he'd mentioned it sooner.'

'Do you? Why?'

It was very cold, but bright, with blue skies turning indigo because the sun was fading fast.

'Isabella always wanted a villa on Lake Garda. Used to go there when she was a child for the summer holidays.'

Leonard's voice was gruff as they looked around to see someone approaching from a long, sleek black car. The driver they had been told to expect. Alessio was meeting them at the villa.

'I always regretted not buying her what she wanted. She could have bought it herself, but she wanted me on board and, fool that I was, I was too wrapped up in work at the time to contemplate a holiday home. A life of little regrets…' He turned to her, watery-eyed. 'And a number of big ones. If I had known that Alessio had bought a place here… It could have been a bridge between us, maybe…a chance to think about things gone by. But enough of this nonsense. Let's appreciate the scenery, my dear!'

They did.

The lights from a huddle of exquisite houses nestled around the glassy lake twinkled in the fading daylight, disappearing up the slopes of the mountains that rose like stern guardians around them.

They sat in companionable silence in the back seat of the luxury car that drove them quietly and swiftly towards their destination. By the time they got there the mountainous backdrop was a dark, brooding mass, and the colourful houses that dotted the water's edge and clambered up the sides of the mountains were shadowy and indistinct.

Leonard was as good as asleep. It had been a long day. He was jostled awake as the sleek car slowed, and even in the gathering gloom they both fell silent at the spectacle that awaited them.

Wide black gates opened automatically, and the car slowly purred up a winding, uphill avenue bordered with trees. In the distance there were lights, and as the car moved on Sophie could see the outline of a magnificent white turreted villa, spectacularly lit against the dark night skies. Behind it, the mountains looked close enough to touch.

'Oh, my...' she breathed.

'I'm impressed,' Leonard murmured next to her, now alert and wide awake.

The front door was opened as the car swung in an arc to park directly outside and there he was, framed in the doorway, the man who had had her nerves skittering for the past few days.

He was dressed in black. Black long-sleeved polo, black jeans. He looked so sexy and so sophisticated that her heart began to hammer and she could only half focus on Leonard.

'Anybody home?' Leonard asked, nudging her.

When she looked at him, his bushy eyebrows were raised, and his eyes slid across to where Alessio was moving towards the car, then back to her flushed face.

'I was just...just...'

'Why don't you help me out, my dear? It's very rude to stare, and you're staring at my son.'

'Yes! Help you out... Of course!'

Sophie's cheeks were on fire. Leonard could see far too much, and he was nowhere near tactful enough for her liking. He had warned her off his son once, and the last thing she needed was for him to get it into his head that she was bothered by Alessio...that she was attracted to him like one of those blondes he always seemed to be photographed with.

Flustered, she could barely meet Alessio's eyes as he neared them, but she was aware of him with every fibre of her being.

'How was the trip?' he asked.

He moved to stand on the other side of Leonard and took his father's left arm as she hooked his right through hers.

'I'm not a complete invalid yet!' Leonard fussed, but he allowed himself to be led into the magnificent house, and as the door closed behind them they both fell silent and looked around.

It was a vision of pale marble, deep rich wood and white walls. The villa stood solitary in its own grounds, surrounded by an army of tall conifers which gave it a serene, otherworldly atmosphere. It was almost as though they had been transported to another planet. Certainly Sophie had never seen anything quite like it, not even in the pages of the most wildly expensive house magazines she had flicked through in the past.

Her eyes drifted to the broad staircase that wound upwards, drawing the gaze to an uber-modern crystal chandelier that fell in a riot of glass teardrops from the ceiling.

The silence stretched, and when Sophie finally finished her inspection and looked at Alessio it was to find him looking right back at her with amusement.

'The trip was fine, thank you,' she said, belatedly answered his question.

Leonard took over, moving forward at a sprightly pace and demanding a full tour of their surroundings, while muttering just loudly enough to be heard that he hoped something like *this* wasn't what he would return to when work had been done on his house.

Alessio responded in good humour and his dark eyes held Sophie's briefly in a wry, conspiratorial look that made her flush. 'I think that I've got the message loud and clear about how little you want things changed.'

'Nothing wrong with that, my boy!' Leonard declared, huffing, and moved on to peer into rooms, taking his time with his inspection.

'We all find our perfect moment in time and stick to it,' Alessio murmured, moving to stand behind his father and towering over him, even though Leonard was by no means a short man.

'Quite right...quite right.'

Standing behind them, and to one side, Sophie wondered what Alessio's perfect moment in time was. Judging from the remote splendour of this villa, she wondered whether he had *ever* found his perfect time. There was certainly nothing personal on display here—nothing that would indicate anything other than a house designed and kitted out to suit a man who had money to burn but no time to relax. But, my, it was an impressive place.

She strolled towards the back of the house, in Leonard's nosy wake, and could make out, through a bank of imposing columns, a wide porch, broad enough to house several sitting areas, and then, down a shallow bank of steps, the faraway glimpse of what looked like a swimming pool.

'Who looks after this place when you're not here, son?' Leonard asked. He had shrugged off Sophie's helping hand and was slowly backtracking his way past the winding staircase towards, she assumed, the kitchen.

'I have a couple who check in daily.'

'Damned waste of money,' Leonard growled, and Sophie, glancing across to Alessio, saw a smile tugging the corners of his mouth.

'I have the money,' he said, without batting an eye, 'so it's my choice what I do with it.'

'Your mother used to come here as a girl,' said Leonard, pushing open another door.

Sure enough, they were in a kitchen the size of a football field. There was more splendid white-blonde wood, and a huge range cooker in brushed steel that seemed madly excessive for a guy with no interest in cooking.

'I know,' Alessio said softly. 'I've seen pictures.'

Father and son exchanged mutually cautious looks and the conversation wasn't developed. Watching from the sidelines, Sophie felt a twinge—a stirring of hope—that bridges might be crossed even though what had happened between them was only her concern insofar as it might or might not affect Leonard's stress levels while he was here.

'The couple', it seemed, did more than look after the house in Alessio's absence. One half of the equation—the husband, as it turned out—was an excellent chef, and they were told he would be preparing all their meals. His wife would take care of the laundry and the cleaning.

'Think it's going to be stress-free enough for my father?' Alessio asked later, when dinner had been eaten and dishes cleared and the practically invisible smiling housekeeper had tidied up behind them.

They had remained in the kitchen. It was as impersonal as the rest of the villa, with none of the clutter of Leonard's kitchen on display. The table was a gleaming granite-topped affair, and Sophie was perched at one end and Alessio at the other. With Leonard no longer in the kitchen with them, she was a little flustered when he shifted to move closer to where she was sitting.

'So…?' he drawled, lazing back in the chair and watching her with close attention. 'I was half expecting the pair of you to stay put.'

'What do you mean?'

'The so-called *pussycat* can be a stubborn mule, and I envisaged him digging his heels in and giving you strict instructions to turn away anyone coming to the door with a bag of tools and some tubs of paint.'

'You're so sarcastic…'

Sophie fiddled with the stem of her wine glass, wanting to peel her eyes away but riveted by his magnetic sex appeal. He had shoved the sleeves of his figure-hugging tee to the elbows, and her eyes disobediently drifted to the silky dark hair on his forearms and the flex of muscle visible under the shirt.

Her throat went dry as he hooked his foot under one of the chairs and dragged it closer, so that he could relax with his feet up on it.

'I'm realistic, Sophie. My father doesn't want anything touched in the house. I appreciate that he wants to keep his memories intact, but I've done my best to persuade him that it would be a pointless exercise if the house ended up going to rack and ruin, at which point the renovations needed would be so extreme that he would have to kiss sweet goodbye to anything being left in place. But I still wasn't convinced he wouldn't backtrack the minute I wasn't around.'

'Well, you must have done a good job of convincing him, because there wasn't a moment when he had any doubts that the work would happen.' She paused and tilted her head to one side. 'In fact, he seems quite content at the moment…even if he's grumbling about everything.' She smiled. 'It's funny, but when I look back on the past few months I can see all the signs of someone who was very anxious. Leonard was quiet when he usually isn't, and there were so many times when I had to say something twice before he even realised that I was speaking to him.'

'My father can be difficult,' Alessio murmured.

'That's not being difficult!' Sophie laughed. 'He had stuff on his mind and no one to share it with.'

'Is this leading up to another criticism of my lack of presence on the scene?'

'No!'

Sophie meant that, and her voice registered surprise. Their eyes tangled and she felt something disturbing flutter inside her, like soft butterfly wings, loosening the muscles between her thighs and making her nipples pinch.

It was a physical, sexual reaction, and for a few seconds she was so horrified and shocked by it that she struggled to get her thoughts together.

This was raw. This was different from objectively looking at him and acknowledging that he was stupidly beautiful.

This was *scary*. Because it wreaked havoc with her self-control, and her self-control was something she took great pride in. She refused to be vulnerable to all those things that could hurt, refused to let go. And this squishy sensation rippling through her felt like letting go and she hated it.

'Anyway,' she said hurriedly, 'I would say that he's a lot less stressed that he was even a couple of weeks ago.'

'Most people like to share their burdens with other people or, even better, have someone else take charge in difficult situations. My father might be opinionated, and he may resent the fact that I've taken over, but he's human, and he'll be relieved that I'm picking up the baton and running with it.'

'I guess you're right...'

Sophie's thoughts drifted to her adolescence, and for a few seconds she tried to imagine what it might have been like if someone else had picked up the baton and run with it.

How different would her life have been?

Without the responsibilities she had shouldered, would she have had the chance to enjoy her teenage years free from gnawing anxiety?

Would that have made her a different person?

Or would she still have been the responsible, sensible one? Was that just the legacy of her birth order? She was the older of two siblings…the one who was always destined to be responsible, whatever the circumstances.

'Penny for them.'

'Sorry?'

Sophie surfaced to find Alessio's dark eyes fixed thoughtfully on her. The overhead lights had been dimmed earlier, on Leonard's orders. They were enjoying a very tasty meal indeed, he'd said. Not trying on clothes in a fitting room where you needed fluorescent lighting to spot every crease in a pair of badly made trousers.

Alessio had left them dimmed, and now the shadows and angles of his face seemed even more forbidding and outrageously sexy.

He was as bronzed as she was fair, and she wondered what their bodies would look like next to one another.

With no clothes on.

She so pale and he so much darker.

The very thought brought hectic colour to her cheeks, and for a couple of seconds she completely forgot what she'd been thinking, and what he had said to interrupt her thoughts.

Her heart sped up, pumping hot blood urgently through her veins, and that squishy feeling coalesced into a need that bloomed inside her. She felt her pant-

...ies dampen and that itch between her thighs...the tingle there that made her want to pass out.

'You're a million miles away. What's going through your head? Negative thoughts about me?'

'It's not all about you,' Sophie said sharply—more sharply than she'd intended. Because her thoughts were all still over the place, making her uncomfortable and defensive with the man who had put them there. 'As a matter of fact I was thinking... I was thinking...'

'Yes? I'm all ears. Tell me what you were thinking.'

He sat forward, and just like that he closed the distance between them, so that she could almost feel the heat emanating from his long, muscular body.

She couldn't escape the suffocating effect he was having on her.

If she kept her eyes on his face she was all too conscious of the depth of his eyes, the lush thickness of eyelashes any woman would have given her eye teeth for, the sensuous mould of his mouth, of the lips that had covered hers...

Looking just a bit lower and the strain of his jeans across his thighs made her feel giddy.

'I was thinking that what you just said...about Leonard being relieved that someone else has taken over... well, you're right. Of course. It's noticeable. It really is. People coping with problems and issues...yes. It's a blessing sometimes when someone steps in...takes over...'

She was stammering, her jerky outpouring of words trying to cover her inner turmoil.

'Not that I would know.'

'You had no one there to help you when you needed help after your father died. Your mother and your sister depended on you and I know you shouldered the burden alone. What about your friends?'

'I don't feel sorry for myself...' she said awkwardly, wishing she had never said anything in the first place.

She focused on what he had said, really giving it consideration. How could she tell him that confiding in anyone about her unhappy situation growing up had felt inappropriate? All her friends had been talking about boys and parties and clothes. Who had wanted to be saddled with her conversation about the cheapest place to buy groceries, or how difficult it sometimes was to deal with her mother when she didn't want to get out of bed? No one.

But Alessio was staring at her, unsmiling, his dark eyes curious, oddly encouraging her to expand on the story she had started.

She thought of the way he had stepped up to the plate. She had been so nervous when she had decided to head to London to see him. She had predetermined that he wasn't going to be obliging, and yet he had put his own life on hold so that he could manage his father's, and he had done so without a single murmur of complaint.

And now here they were, in this stunning villa, and arrangements had been made for Leonard's house to be renovated. And she knew that Alessio had taken a personal interest in finding out just what his father wanted, had allayed all his doubts and fears and done so without resentment.

So...?

As they sat there in the kitchen, Sophie felt the strangest temptation to break all her rules and open herself up in ways she wasn't accustomed to doing.

'Talk to me, Sophie,' Alessio murmured.

He dropped his feet to the ground and leaned towards her, his arms resting loosely on his thighs, his knees almost but not quite touching hers.

'Don't be silly.' Her voice was shaky when she replied, and she was held captive by his calm, unwavering stare. 'Since when are you interested in listening to what I have to say about anything that isn't to do with your father? Besides, I've already told you about…about my mother and my sister. There's no need to pretend any more interest.'

'Now who's being silly…?'

'Alessio…' She threaded her fingers through her spiky fair hair and darted a helpless look at him.

'*Alessio*… I like the way you say my name… You have a husky voice—has anyone ever told you that?'

'Is that a compliment?'

She smiled. Her pulses were racing. There was a simmering, sizzling excitement zigzagging just below the surface that felt dangerous but compelling at the same time. And she didn't know whether she was imagining it or not…didn't quite know what to do with it.

'It is. It makes it sound as though you think carefully about every word that leaves your mouth.'

This time she laughed and relaxed. 'Don't most people think before they speak?'

'You'd be surprised…'

'What do you mean?'

Alessio grinned crookedly and raked his fingers through his hair without taking his eyes off her face for a second.

Sophie's breath caught in her throat and she blinked, because for a moment she could see the boy behind the man, and the humour that made him so much more than an aggressively talented billionaire who was feared and respected in equal measure.

'I *mean*,' Alessio said, 'that most of the women I go out with talk a lot, and in very high, urgent voices. A lot of them seem to feel that their mission should be to cram as many words in as they can before pausing for breath.'

'That's mean.' But she hitched a low laugh.

'I exaggerate. But only slightly.'

'They probably talk a lot because they're trying to impress you.'

'And of course that's the last thing *you* would ever think of doing...'

'The very last thing,' Sophie breathed, lowering her eyes.

'So now we've established that, believe me when I tell you that I'm interested in what you have to say. And I'll tell you something else... You and my dad...' He shook his head, and smiled and shrugged at the same time. 'I never realised how entwined your lives were.'

'I do work for him on a full-time basis...'

Alessio smiled softly. 'My extremely dedicated PA works for me full-time. Our lives are far from entwined.'

Sophie grimaced. 'I suppose to start with, when we were still getting to know one another, it was a more formal arrangement. We had a rigid schedule for pretty much everything. But it wasn't long before...'

'Before my father started pushing the boundaries like a toddler?'

Sophie laughed. 'He *can* be quite mischievous sometimes.'

Their gazes met and held. Was she aware of how exciting she was?

No, she wasn't.

Looking at her, Alessio knew that she had no idea how invigorating it was for him to converse with a woman who wasn't out to impress him. It wasn't just the tenor of her voice that he liked, but the substance behind what she said. She was so different from the women he dated that she could have been from another planet.

There was no name-dropping...no flirting...no thrilling anecdotes about exciting parties where so-and-so had been chatting to so-and-so and you'd never guess who was there...

She was...bloody refreshing.

And he was enjoying more than just their conversation.

He was enjoying the play of emotions that crisscrossed her face and her responses to what he said—some of which he could tell she was trying hard to downplay.

He was enjoying the way she blushed, because he didn't have much experience of women who did that.

Because he only went for a certain type of woman.

That was the thought that registered on the outer edges of his brain as he continued to look at the woman sitting opposite him, admiring the smoothness of her skin, the intelligence in her eyes, the girlish disingenuity and the strength beyond her years that blended into an intriguing mix.

Was it her novelty that he found so captivating all of a sudden?

Of course it was.

What else?

Alessio's work life was high-octane, so he had always liked the predictability of women who didn't stress him. He didn't want to have to deal with shrewish demands or hissy fits. His life might not be free of them completely, but in truth his interactions with the opposite sex were not rollercoaster rides.

After a long hard day at work, who wanted a rollercoaster ride?

In fact, who wanted a rollercoaster ride with anyone? Ever? Certainly not Alessio. As far as he was concerned, emotional rollercoaster rides were for fools who allowed their hearts to dictate their behaviour.

He would never be that person. He would never allow his heart to get in the way of anything. He would never open himself to the pain of loss because he had learnt from a young age that love and loss were entwined. He had loved his mother and he had lost her, and it had driven him half-crazy as a kid.

And he had loved his father and lost him as well. Not in the physical sense, but emotionally. Because his father had withdrawn into a world that had excluded him,

Alessio. He had shut the door and that door had never been reopened. The lock on it had just grown rustier over time…harder to break.

So self-control always lay at the heart of Alessio's dealings with women. And if this happened to be one of those rare instances when his self-control was missing in action, then he knew that there was nothing to worry about.

Why would there be?

Curiosity flared. What sort of guys did Sadie go for anyway? Tall? Short? Thin? Fat? What fish in the sea took her fancy? He wanted to find out more about her, and he liked the novelty of that.

At the receiving end of those dark, speculative, brooding eyes, Sophie felt the rush of nerves. Her body urged her to move forward, to let herself be absorbed by his powerful, charismatic personality. But her brain took fright and she jerked back. Her hand whipped to the side and a wine glass shattered at the sudden impact.

Was it instinct or distraction that made her reach out to try and save it at just the wrong moment?

She pulled her hand away with a cry, and when she looked at her palm she could see a shard of glass caught there…more than one shard.

Everything had happened in the blink of an eye, but before she could do anything Alessio had her hand in his and was staring at the droplets of blood.

'Sit still.'

'I'm fine.'

'I need to get the glass out. The last thing you want is an infection to set in.'

'Alessio,' Sophie said faintly, 'honestly… I can deal with this…'

But he was already heading to one of the cupboards, to return seconds later with a First Aid box and a bottle of spirit.

She fell silent as he gently took her hand in his and began dealing with the cut. The glass was onlt skin-deep. She hadn't caught it with enough strength for it to have penetrated. He was meticulous, and as he worked he talked to her in a low, melodious voice that was soothing, and relaxing, and knocked back all the barriers that had been in place.

He joked that the First Aid box was about the only thing he could locate fast in the kitchen, because he'd had to sit through a tutorial on how to use the contents when the housekeeper had bought it. He described the lake, which could be accessed from his massive garden down a series of winding steps. He talked about the boat he had which was seldom used because time never seemed to be on his side.

Without her noticing, he had moved to kneel at her feet, and she watched his dark head and the careful delicacy of his fingers as bit by bit he cleaned the tear in her skin.

Sophie wanted to laugh, and make a wisecrack about not knowing that he was a trained doctor along with everything else, but she was mesmerised by him, stilled by the touch of his hand on hers. Her heart was thumping against her ribcage, and she could feel the silence in the kitchen like something weighty and tangible.

He wrapped a bandage around her palm and expertly secured it, but when he finally met her eyes he didn't move away, back to his chair.

He remained where he was, and her mouth parted and her breath hitched in her throat, because there was an intent in his dark eyes that fired something similar in her.

Naked *want*—the very same want she had tried so hard to lock away, where it couldn't do any harm—was out of its cage now and bringing wild colour to her cheeks.

She wasn't surprised when he straightened up to curve his hand against the side of her flushed face. She angled herself against it and felt her eyelids flutter.

Last time when he had kissed her, sanity had come roaring back at speed.

This time, as she leaned towards him and gently covered his mouth with hers, she wanted to let herself go.

She'd never done that. She had no idea what it felt like to be swept away on a tide of longing and she wanted to find out.

What was wrong with that?

She kissed him.

She was vaguely aware of them shifting positions and wasn't sure how it had happened. But suddenly he had moved from ground to chair, and she had shifted from her chair to his lap, was straddling him and gently rocking as they continued to kiss.

Her panties were wet, soaked, and she rolled her hips

so that she could press against him, relieving some of the urgent ache between her legs.

He groaned as she kissed his face, his neck, stroked his shoulders and felt the hard bulge of muscle under his stretchy tee shirt.

She was barely aware of the hindrance of her bandaged hand because her body was on fire.

His hand stole up to cup her breast and then slid underneath her top, and she shuddered and arched her back, urging him to do more than just caress her.

She hissed a sigh and moaned when he shoved the top up, his hand shaking as he unclasped her bra and then pushed that up as well.

Small, perfect breasts.

Alessio had never felt such a loss of his prized self-control in his life before. But the sight of her bare breasts, her blushing pink nipples, fired him up to such a frenzy of response that he was on the brink of losing it completely and ejaculating prematurely.

Unthinkable.

He darted his tongue to flick the stiffened bud of one nipple, and then took it into his mouth and suckled.

Hands on her shoulders, he angled her so that he could enjoy her.

The more he tasted, the more he wanted to taste.

Not just her breasts…not just her nipples.

Alessio wanted to explore every inch of her exquisite body and then, when he'd done that, he wanted to start all over again.

'My bedroom?' he growled, drawing back to look at her.

'Alessio…' Sophie breathed, drowsily meeting his hot stare.

'There's no pressure, Sophie…' he told her.

He contemplated the gut-wrenching disappointment of a long and very cold shower, should she change her mind, but if she did, then that was her right and he would respect it.

'I want this, Alessio…'

'Are you quite sure?' He paused and tangled his fingers in her short, fair hair. 'Is this what you want? I can't offer permanence…'

'I know that.' Sophie smiled. 'For your information, neither can I…'

'So, my bedroom?'

'Your bedroom,' she agreed with pleasurable abandon, as he lost himself in her smile.

CHAPTER SEVEN

SOPHIE GAZED AT ALESSIO, her eyes half closed and feeling greedy with longing. The villa was quiet and in darkness because it was a little after eleven. The couple who worked there had disappeared ages ago, and Leonard was safely tucked away in his bedroom fast asleep.

In front of her Alessio stood, magnificently bare-chested. Low-slung jeans, unbuttoned, rode low on his lean hips. He had tossed his sweater on the ground, and with his hand resting loosely on the zipper of his jeans was ready to complete the job of getting undressed.

Four days...

That was how long these clandestine liaisons had been happening.

They had made love on that first night, after tiptoeing up the stairs, making sure not to wake Leonard, and it had been the most mind-blowing experience Sophie had ever had.

He had touched her in places that had made her melt, had licked and explored with his tongue and his mouth until she had groaned low and deep, barely recognising her own gasps of pleasure.

She had gone from cautious to addicted at supersonic speed, and it had been tacitly and wordlessly decided that their first experience was not going to be their last.

How long it was going to last, Sophie had no idea. Not beyond this stay at his villa on the lake. She'd assumed that. Relationships didn't last with Alessio, and this one, which was out of the ordinary, would definitely have a cut-off to it that would be shorter than usual.

She was no pliable, dependent, clingy, sexy little blonde thing. She answered back. And she felt he didn't encourage that in the women he dated, even though he'd told her that he liked that trait in her.

She was also trying hard to build on the slender foundations she could see being re-erected between him and his father, and whenever he frowned and looked at her in a way that said *You're going beyond your brief,* she simply stared back at him with feigned innocence and refused to back off.

He never snapped, and she thought that was because he was enjoying himself too much to risk her taking offence and turning her back on him.

'Sex has never felt so good,' he'd told her only the night before.

With Alessio, it was all about the sex. He had a high libido and a hunger for her that was flattering and compulsive.

Only now and again did she feel a twinge of sadness that everything began and ended with the physical—although that was a reaction she didn't stop to think about, because she told herself that it was the same for her.

He was vital and sexy and erotic, and he was opening her up to a world of experience she had been denied.

She wasn't in it for any kind of gooey-eyed, hand-holding relationship. He wasn't her type.

She could never give her heart to anyone who wasn't prepared to look after it, and Alessio wasn't the kind of guy who signed up for looking after a woman's heart.

'Sometimes,' he drawled, now, snapping her out of her thoughts, 'I look at you and you're a thousand miles away. Where are you? Different place? Different country?' He delivered a wicked smile. 'Just as long as the man you're with there is me, then I don't care...'

He unzipped the trousers and Sophie hitched herself up onto her elbows and watched his smile broaden.

He knew she liked watching him.

She'd told him that it turned her on. Just as it turned him on for her to be naked when she watched, so that he could see her body, waiting in readiness for him to pleasure it.

She was naked now, lying on the king-sized bed in his enormous bedroom, which was a marvel of pale colours, dark wood and lots of hidden cupboards that slid open at the push of a button.

Like in every other room in his magnificent villa, the minimalist paleness of everything made Sophie think that this was a place no one under the age of eighteen should ever be brought—just in case sticky fingers or spillages ruined the pristine perfection. This was an adults-only escape, from the hard beauty of the marble to the bold abstracts hanging on the walls and, outside, the exquisite infinity pool which was surrounded by pruned trees and would doubtless come into its own during the warmer months.

In a playground for the rich and famous, Alessio's villa was right up there with the most dazzling.

The evening before, after Leonard had retired for the night, he had taken her out into the garden, with its lawns clipped to precise perfection, and led her down a bank of stone steps, romantically lit with small twinkling lights. They had led to his very own sprawling deck that accessed the lake. They had stood looking over the glassy dark beauty of the water and it had been magical. Crisp and cold and absolutely perfect.

Was it any wonder that she sometimes felt as helpless as a moth, dazzled by the force of a flame that shone brighter than anything she could ever have imagined?

She gazed at him, so beautiful in the shadows of darkness. His jeans joined his sweater on the ground, and then the dark boxers, and her breath caught sharply at his proud erection, which he briefly circled with his hand before moving towards her.

Sophie half closed her eyes and touched her breast, then traced the contour of her nipple with her finger. On top of the duvet, completely naked, she let her legs fall apart, encouraging a look of hot desire from Alessio as he joined her on the bed.

'I like what I see,' he murmured, lying next to her on his side, pressed against her so that she could feel the throb of his erection at her thigh.

'What's that?' Sophie curved to face him so that they were eye to eye, her belly touching his.

She lifted her leg to cover his thigh, and then manoeuvred her body so that she could rub her wetness against him. She shuddered and closed her eyes when he gently stroked her nipple with his finger, picking up where she had left off and tracing the outline before homing in on the stiffened bud.

'Are you going to tell me what you were thinking?' he murmured, licking his finger before replacing it on her nipple, so that he could dampen it into even more sensitivity.

'I wasn't thinking anything.'

'Now, why don't I believe you?'

He nuzzled the side of her neck, her jawline, peppering her with the lightest of feathery kisses that made her want to squirm and wriggle against him.

He was the consummate lover.

He knew how to touch her and where… He knew how to get her to fever pitch and then take her even higher. He could make her body feel in ways she had never imagined possible.

Yet Sophie knew the limits of what they had—just as she knew that telling him what was going through her head would be a mistake of biblical proportions.

Because what had got into her that suddenly she was thinking ahead?

Why was she beginning to wonder what it might feel like when this ended amicably?

She'd jumped in, wide eyes open, and hadn't even bothered to think ahead to how they might rub along when they returned to England.

Of course he would go back to London. And she and

Leonard would once again resume their daily routine. But how was that going to feel after *this*?

'I have no idea why you don't believe me,' she said, kissing him softly to extinguish a conversation she didn't want to have.

He smiled against her mouth.

'Because you're not a woman whose mind is ever empty of thoughts.'

Their eyes tangled. For a few seconds Alessio was side-swiped by the oddest notion that he *wanted* to find out what she had been thinking...what had put that remote expression in her eyes.

Why?

He *never* felt the slightest temptation to second-guess what was going through any woman's head. That wasn't what he was about.

But for no reason, the compulsion to know what *she* was thinking was overwhelming.

'I'll take that as a compliment,' Sophie murmured.

Having never been given the brush-off before, Alessio took a couple of seconds to actually recognise the sound of it, and when he did he had to force himself to take it on the chin, because the last thing he needed was some kind of deep and meaningful conversation that would end up going nowhere.

Did it matter what she was thinking?

It was almost laughable that he had momentarily been so invested in finding out!

'So you should,' he said. 'But enough talk...'

They made love.

His mind emptied as he touched her. His curiosity to get inside her head fell away as he skimmed her slender body with his hand, pausing to cup her breasts and tease her rosebud nipples.

She arched up, and he knew what she wanted and was happy to oblige. More than happy.

He took one pulsing pink nipple into his mouth and lost himself in the taste and feel of it as he sucked, while he teased her other breast with his hand.

He went slowly.

That first time they had made love he had been so turned on that he'd rushed, hadn't given her the attention she deserved, but he had made up for that since then.

True, the days passed agonisingly slowly, with only the occasional touch, the brush of his fingers accidentally against hers... True, by the time his father was safely asleep he was so keyed up he could barely think straight... But even so he always made sure never to rush when they were finally in bed.

He let his hand drift lazily over her slender body, tracing every inch, feathering over her ribcage, dipping down to her belly button and then edging to the soft downy fluff between her legs.

He parted her thighs, felt the wetness between them, and struggled to hold on to the urge to go faster.

He slipped his finger inside and then trailed his lips downwards as he played with her, teasing the tightened bud of her clitoris and enjoying the way she squirmed against his finger.

* * *

Sophie's eyelids fluttered.

Knowing what he was going to do didn't reduce the thrill of excitement and anticipation that flooded through her.

She tensed, feeling his mouth teasing her, and then groaned, low and soft, when his tongue slid to tickle her clitoris. She let her legs drop, enjoyed him pleasuring her, and then took charge to change the equation.

She heard his full-throated chuckle as she manoeuvred him as expertly as he manoeuvred her, so that she could enjoy and pleasure *him* just exactly as he had been enjoying and pleasuring *her*.

She tasted him as he had tasted her, in a mutual giving to one another that made her feel warm and so fulfilled inside.

Alessio was the first to break their embrace, growling that any more and he would go flying off the edge.

She laughed, and then groaned again when he thrust into her, long and deep, moving slowly at first, then speeding up, his own guttural moans mirroring hers.

Sophie's orgasm ripped through her, stiffening her and then sending her into a spiral of satisfaction that seemed to go on and on until she was finally spent.

They curled into one another, bodies slick with perspiration, and she nuzzled against him.

Alessio felt the warmth of her face pressed against his neck, felt the way she burrowed like a little rabbit, and something very much like peace settled in him, filling every part of him.

He toyed with her hair, asked her whether she'd ever had it long, smiled when she told him she'd always just liked the ease of short hair.

So like her.

So unfussy.

So suddenly scary.

This was nothing that Alessio had ever felt before. He could have stayed right there…with her so soft against him…for ever.

A perfect moment.

And one that he wasn't going to allow. Letting his body guide him, feeling compelled to touch, was one thing. Lust was instinctive, and even if this felt raw and wild, he knew that it was nothing that could threaten his self-control. In the end, he could put lust right back in its box, close the lid and walk away.

Hadn't he done just that, many, many times before?

So what if this felt different? He had already worked out that it was down to the novelty value. He'd been knocked sideways by an attraction he hadn't seen coming. He'd assumed one thing about the woman snuggled against him, only to find that all his assumptions had been wrong.

Therein lay this weakness now, and it was a weakness that went against every single principle he had ever held dear.

No attachment. No vulnerability. No *caring*.

This felt suspiciously like all three.

No question, he was off target with this, but he'd always been a guy who believed in the motto that it was better to be safe than sorry.

He stiffened, edged himself apart from her—just fractionally, but enough to convey a message. And of course she read that message, loud and clear, and likewise detached herself, with a breathless little laugh that was half awkward, half embarrassed.

Just the sort of laugh he wanted to kiss away.

He clenched his jaw and fought down everything in him that was in danger of softening.

'I'm suddenly thirsty,' he said abruptly. 'Think I'll head downstairs for some water...'

Sophie pulled back as though she'd been stung. She knew what this was about. Just for a second she had utterly relaxed against him, had wrapped herself around him and cuddled him, and he had shot back, his immediate and instinctive response to repel any such intimacy.

Sex was hot and hard and rapturously enjoyable. But cuddles? Tenderness? Those were things that were very different, and he was making sure that she noted the distinction...making sure she didn't get ideas into her head that this was anything more than it actually was.

A time-limited fling between two very different people.

It hurt.

It hurt because she'd gone and invested more into this non-relationship than she'd dreamt possible. It hurt because she'd clung in a way she'd never planned on clinging. And now he'd sensed it and pulled back because it wasn't what he wanted.

'Sex is thirsty business!'

She injected airiness into her voice and hoicked herself up on her elbows as he swung his beautiful body off the mattress, padding around in the semi-darkness to grab whatever discarded clothes he could put his hands on.

Sophie stared from under lowered lashes, her eyes adjusting to the darkness and making out his silhouette and the grace of his body as he slung on the jeans he had earlier thrown off in his urgency to join her on the bed.

He wasn't looking at her at all.

He spun round but only half turned when his hand was on the doorknob, to ask her if he could bring her anything.

'I think I'll head back to my room,' she said casually. But really she was waiting for him to leave, suddenly conscious of her nudity.

Alessio didn't say anything, then he nodded and shrugged and turned to open the door, letting in a stream of light that surely shouldn't have been there, because they were always really careful to switch all the lights off in the wide corridor.

Leonard's room was at the end of the corridor, and they had become accustomed to stealth—the trademark of the clandestine affair.

She heard Leonard before she saw him—heard him booming to Alessio that he had heard voices, had been worried that someone might have broken in.

Alessio's voice, in return, was cool and confident

and amused as he reassured his father that the house was safer than a bank vault.

'I have so many well-positioned CCTV cameras that not even the Invisible Man could get past them. So there's no need for you to trouble yourself. It's late. Let me escort you back to your bedroom...'

'Hang on just a minute, my boy!'

Sophie cringed in horror as she heard Leonard bang on the door with his walking stick.

Old and in questionable health he might be, but he still had a formidable amount of stamina when it came to making his presence felt.

He pushed the door wide open before Alessio could do anything to stop him and before Sophie could take evasive action.

Although what would that evasive action have been?

Lunging for a cupboard? Ducking underneath the bed? Making a run for the bathroom and locking the door behind her?

Ridiculous.

She drew the covers right up to her chin, pulled her knees up and watched as Leonard slowly shuffled his way into the bedroom and switched on the overhead light.

'I knew it!' he roared, spinning around to glare at Alessio, who was hovering in the doorway, the very picture of embarrassment.

The fact that he was half naked said it all.

She had never seen him as ill at ease as he was now, indecisive as he leant against the doorframe, raking his fingers through his hair before folding his arms and staring at Leonard, deprived of speech for once.

'How the hell long has this been going on?' Leonard bellowed into the silence.

'Dad…'

'Don't you *Dad* me!'

He tapped his way over to the bed and sat heavily on it while Sophie tried to remember how to breathe.

'I expected better of you,' he told her mournfully, turning his back to Alessio, who was still hovering in the doorway. 'Alessio…' He waved one hand dismissively towards his son without looking around. 'I know that boy and his philandering ways.' He narrowed his eyes on Sophie and looked at her with a shrewd stare. 'Seduced you, did he? Took advantage? I could see you had eyes for him.'

'Leonard…' She felt faint.

'I'm seeing it all clearly now, my dear,' he continued shakily. 'Used his charms on you…turned your head. Seduced you.' At this he cast a baleful glance over his shoulder.

Sophie met Alessio's dark gaze and knew in that instant that he would say nothing in receipt of this slander. He would consider her, consider the relationship she had with his father, which had always been based on fondness, affection and trust, and he would respect it enough to back away from making a stand for himself. He would take the hit.

'It's not like that…' Sophie muttered, beetroot-red.

'Speak up, my dear. I'm old and hard of hearing.'

Sophie knew that Leonard's hearing was as sharp as her own, but he had been confronted with a horror story and he wasn't going to let either her or Alessio off the hook.

In an instant she realised just how deep her affection for this difficult but lovable old man was. The thought of his disappointment cut her to the quick, but there was no way she was going to let his son take the rap for this.

She wished that she was at least having this conversation fully dressed, instead of huddled in mortified nakedness under the duvet.

'It wasn't your son's fault…' She cleared her throat.

'Come again?'

'I said…it just…*happened*, Leonard. Neither of us planned it and Alessio didn't…didn't seduce me…'

Sophie knew how helpless she sounded.

How could falling into bed with a guy who was off-limits *just happen*? Especially when you considered that they'd never had much to do with one another in all the time she'd worked for Leonard.

Was it any wonder that he was now staring at her, open-mouthed? With a look that was a mixture of incredulity and dismay?

That didn't last long, because he immediately stood up, spun on his heel and banged his walking stick on the floor a couple of times.

'You took advantage of her,' he accused.

He tottered towards the chair just beyond the bed and slumped heavily into it. He looked exhausted.

It was late. A combination of weariness and heightened stimulation was gaining momentum, turning his face waxy and ashen.

Alarmed, and with her nursing instincts coming into play, Sophie lunged off the bed, making sure to drag the sheets around her, and staggered to get her balance before retrieving her scattered clothes from the floor, while issuing orders for Alessio to fetch some water.

She went to the ensuite bathroom and flung on her clothes—jeans and a loose tee shirt. No bra. No underwear. No time.

Leonard was still in the chair and barely glanced at her as she moved quickly towards him.

'Leonard…'

'Alessio should have known better!'

'You can't blame your son.'

'I can and I do.'

'Why?'

'Because I *know* you, Sophie. You're not that type of girl.'

'What type of girl is that?'

'You know what type,' Leonard said quietly. 'You don't throw yourself around. You're a homebody. You enjoy being still, not racing through life seeing who you can sleep with.'

'Good Lord, Leonard.' Sophie smiled gently. 'I'm really not sure I like the person you're describing. She sounds very dull.'

'She's not.' Leonard smiled back weakly and reached

out to squeeze her hand. 'She's a kind person who's very dear to me, and that's why I blame Alessio for this.'

Leonard rested back into the chair and closed his eyes.

'He's a love 'em and leave 'em man, and that's just fine and dandy. But not when it concerns you, my dear.'

Sophie didn't say anything.

Leonard looked drained.

His doctor had said no stress, and she hadn't seen him this stressed in all the time she had known him.

'We should probably get back to bed.'

Sophie swung round, craning her neck to see Alessio standing behind her where she had positioned herself on a squat upholstered stool in front of Leonard.

'How the hell do you expect me to sleep, Alessio'

'Here, drink some of this water.'

'Sophie is trying to make me believe that this was some kind of…mutual understanding between the pair of you! But I know you, Alessio, and she's not one of your…your *trollops*!'

'No, she certainly isn't one of those,' Alessio murmured, dragging a chair over so that he and Sophie were now on either side of Leonard.

'You can't have one of those "mutual understandings" with her!'

'Leonard!' Sophie protested. 'Believe it or not, I can have any amount of mutual understandings that I want! I'm a big girl!'

Was she, though?

Uttering those words had brought a wave of confusion. If she really was a big girl, up for 'mutual understandings', then why was she becoming so conflicted about what she and Alessio had started in good faith?

Why had she suddenly found herself wanting *more*?

She was terrified of clinging to him. She knew, and had known from the start, all the limitations that came with this relationship.

If it could even be called a relationship!

Certainly, Leonard would beg to differ!

But common sense was no longer functioning, so how, exactly, did that non-functioning common sense back up what she had said about being a big girl?

'I'd planned on talking to you tomorrow about this,' Alessio was saying softly to his father, at which Leonard seemed to perk up a little.

Sophie frowned at him. 'You had?'

'You've probably forgotten. Yesterday was a busy day. Walking into town…having lunch by the lake… taking my father out on a boat despite his protests…'

'It was a very busy day,' Sophie said vaguely, trying hard to work out when she and Alessio were supposed to have had this conversation about him having a conversation with his father.

She guessed that it might be possible. Sometimes when she was with him everything seemed to leave her head in a whoosh…every single thought.

Factor in the fact that she was in just about one of the most picturesque places on the planet, and she could surely be forgiven for overlooking the occasional discussion. Who wouldn't forget the odd chat when they were out on a glittering turquoise lake, staring back at colourful houses, an orderly jumble of pastel Lego, as picture-perfect as anything she had ever seen?

Except…

The way he was staring at her now, with his dark eyes warm and…*complicit*…

'Remember I told you that I would be telling my father about us?'

Sophie opened her mouth, because if Alessio had come close to saying anything like that, then there was no question that the conversation would have been lodged at the very top of her mind, picture-perfect scenery or no picture-perfect scenery.

'Telling him that what we have…' Alessio's voice was husky and he reached out and took her fingers in his '…is serious stuff…'

'What are you saying, my boy?' Leonard piped up, temporarily drowning out the clamour of stunned confusion in Sophie's head.

'I'm saying, Dad, that this isn't what you think it is.'

Alessio held up his hand, briefly giving Sophie time to recover from the slow burn his entwined fingers had been arousing in her. He gestured with a mixture of ruefulness and sincerity.

'Hmph…'

'You think I've been turning Sophie's head…'

'Can you blame me?'

'I don't suppose I can. You've probably seen all the media coverage. Paparazzi always seem to lurk round every corner when I have a woman on my arm…'

'You've never made it a priority to keep a low profile, Alessio,' Leonard said testily, but his mood had changed. His colour was back and there was a brightness in his eyes that hadn't been there before.

Sophie was listening to this exchange in growing bewilderment. Where was Alessio going with this? Her brain was struggling to join the dots, even though somewhere inside she knew that the dots were easy enough to join.

Leonard had caught them *in flagrante delicto*...

He had become stressed...

His consultant had told them that he shouldn't be stressed because it might lead to a recurrence of his health problems...

And so Alessio had leapt in with a solution he thought would do the trick.

It was easy to figure out, and yet Sophie recoiled from that obvious conclusion—just couldn't make sense of it.

Her heart was racing as she sat in dumbfounded silence. Thankfully, Leonard's attention was riveted on Alessio. If he had glanced in her direction he might have been bemused by her stunned expression.

She surfaced to hear Alessio reassuring his father that he was a changed man. His hand returned to hold hers in a show of loving unity, and when he gently squeezed it she had no need to glance at his face to know what he was telling her... *Go with me on this.*

She would.

For Leonard's sake...

But she could feel a low-level anger buzzing inside her, growing stronger with every passing second.

'Trust me, Dad,' Alessio murmured, reaching out

to pat his father's arm. 'Sophie is different from all the women I've ever dated in the past, and I'm asking you to believe me when I tell you that what we have is nothing like anything I've had in my life before.' Dark eyes slid across to Sophie's face. 'I'm a different man when I'm with her...'

'And this turnaround has all happened in the space of a few days?'

Leonard's attention had shifted to Sophie, who was horrified to be the cynosure of his attention.

He had eagle eyes, and he was as sharp as a tack when it came to ferreting out stuff she might prefer to keep to herself.

'We...er...' Sophie licked her lips and smiled weakly. 'Er...well, you know how it is, Leonard,' she mumbled. 'It just sort of happened...'

She held her breath and waited for a barrage of disbelief. How could someone as switched-on as Leonard, who was so cynical about Alessio, do anything but scoff at the preposterous suggestion that in the space of a few days an inveterate womaniser had changed his spots?

Nothing came.

Sophie nervously looked at him and wondered how else she might expand without giving herself away. But she didn't have to say a word, because he reached forward and covered her hand with his.

His eyes were watery. Was he about to cry because of the horror of the situation?

Sophie opened her mouth to say something, *anything*, but before she could get there he was telling her, softly, that he understood.

'It was the same for me,' he said whimsically. 'One look at Isabella and she was the one. That mistake that happened afterwards...' He looked at Alessio with a direct stare. 'I was lonely and heartbroken and a fool, and I should have known better.' He reached out and patted Alessio's hand. 'You've made me a very happy man, son.'

He began to heave himself to his feet.

Sophie was numb. She remained where she was as Alessio rushed to help his father. She watched, dimly aware of Leonard still talking as they headed out of the bedroom.

Talking about what?

She shuddered to think.

She would wait for Alessio and then find out what the heck happened next...

CHAPTER EIGHT

ALESSIO REAPPEARED TWENTY minutes later, by which time Sophie had headed down to the kitchen, leaving in her wake a trail of breadcrumbs for him to follow in the form of lights switched on, on the landing, down the grand staircase, and in the broad corridor that led to the kitchen.

Tense as a bowstring, eyes peeled on the door, she straightened when he pushed open the door and entered the room.

'Clear path to follow to find you here,' he said wryly, following her lead and making himself a cup of coffee. 'All the lights on.'

'What's going on, Alessio?' Sophie asked quietly.

She cradled her mug and watched as he took his time making the coffee, helplessly sucked in by his masculine beauty, the economic grace of his movements as he stirred his drink and returned the milk to the fridge, before swinging round to look at her.

He leaned against the kitchen counter in silence for a few seconds, as though marshalling his thoughts. Then,

'You're…taken aback…' he began, at which Sophie gave a dry bark of laughter.

'*Taken aback*, Alessio? *Taken aback* is when something you're expecting in the post arrives a day late! I'm not *taken aback*. I'm…utterly bewildered at what happened just then.'

'You know what happened.'

Alessio padded across to the table where she was sitting and sat on the chair closest to her, adjusting it so that they were directly facing one another.

Sophie's body instantly responded to his proximity, primed to be turned on the second he was within touching distance of her.

She realised, with dismay, just how vulnerable she had let herself become. She had gone from cautious to smitten in record time and she could have kicked herself.

How could she have known Alessio for what he was and still allowed herself to be bowled over by his charm? His wit? His intelligence? His sex appeal?

How could she have moved so swiftly from a position of self-defence to a place where she'd laid down her arms and thrown down a welcome mat?

Leonard had rushed to conclude that his son had been the seducer, but Sophie recognised with painful honesty that she had practically flung herself at him.

She blinked, dragged herself back to the present, and focused on the man sitting so close to her now—close enough for his unique masculine scent to waft over her, making her heart skip a beat.

Disastrously, he reached for her hand and linked his

fingers lightly with hers as he proceeded to stare at her with earnest honesty.

'Alessio…'

'I know what happened might have been a little un-expected…'

'To say the least.'

'But when I saw my father on the landing…realised that he had probably woken up and heard a noise from the bedroom when he was on his way to the kitchen for God only knows what reason…well, I had to think on my feet…'

'But how could lying to him have been a good idea?'

'There was no alternative.'

'There's *always* an alternative to lying, Alessio.'

He had the grace to flush, but there was determination in his dark eyes as he held her stare.

'Yes, there is. Of course there is. But let's consider that alternative.'

Sophie stared down at their entwined fingers. If she had spent the past few days on a rollercoaster ride, then it now felt as though that ride had sprouted wings and was flying off into orbit at the speed of light.

In her head, she kept seeing Leonard's face when he had looked at her. She had sensed the disappointment and recoiled from it, but *lying*?

Alessio's voice was low and hypnotic, and she remained silent as he gazed at her. 'The main thing to consider is my father's health. Would you agree?'

'Yes, of course. But all the same…'

'When he clocked what was happening—that you

were in my bedroom—his face went ashen. I thought he was going to keel over.'

'He must have been shocked to the core,' Sophie said jerkily, on the verge of tears. 'He might have been big in business, and he might have been through two marriages, but there's a side to him that's very traditional.'

Alessio opened his mouth to contradict that, to point out that however traditional his father might be he was fully aware of the bees and the birds and what happened between a man and a woman when mutual attraction decided to strike.

But then it hit him that Sophie saw a different side to his father, a gentler side, and if she *thought* that he was traditional, then perhaps what she saw was an old man who *was* deeply traditional.

Alessio was one hundred per cent sure that if his father had interrupted him with one of his string of blondes reclining in rumpled disarray in his bed, he would have snorted in resigned disgust and moved on.

But Sophie was different.

He had put her on a pedestal, had formed a bond with her that was paternal and protective—hence his appalled horror at what had been a perfectly natural situation.

More or less...

'He did seem shocked,' Alessio conceded.

'You could have just shut the door firmly behind you.'

'It *was* shut, Sophie. He heard voices. He put two and two together. There's only three of us in this villa, so it really didn't take him long to work out what was going on.'

'We should never have started this,' Sophie whispered.

'It's too late to go down that road. We were caught red-handed, and I knew in that moment that I had to spare my father the stress of thinking that you had become one of my conquests. In case you haven't noticed, his opinion of my love-life leaves a lot to be desired.'

'Yes,' Sophie muttered, thinking back to the many times Leonard had passed caustic remarks about the women his son chose to date and the speed of turnover.

'He… It would have been different if he had interrupted me with another woman…' Alessio raked his fingers through his hair and tilted her chin so that she was forced to look at him. 'But he sees you as his… Well, in some ways as the daughter he never had, and as such he's very protective of you.'

'Yes, but…'

'But nothing, Sophie. He got himself into a state, thinking that I might hurt you…'

'The way you hurt other women?'

'I don't hurt other women. I have fun with them, and they have fun with me, and I treat them very well along the way.' Alessio scowled. 'Besides, we've been over this. I suppose I could have sat him down and told him that we entered into this from the same starting point, that we're both adults who know what we're doing, but in the heat of the moment the only thing I wanted to do was reassure him.'

'I suppose I can appreciate that.'

She sighed. Was it idealistic to think that telling the truth was always the better idea? And since when could she hold herself up as a paragon of virtue on that front?

When she cast her mind back, wouldn't she think of times when she had bent the truth to spare her mother undue worry? When she'd told her that everything was going to be fine? That the money was all okay? That the teachers were thrilled with Addy's work? That she was working after school now and again for fun, and not because they were desperate for the cash?

That life was just fine and there was nothing to angst about?

So who was she to start preaching now?

Of course when he was presented with the unexpected Alessio was going to do his best to smooth things out. And wasn't that a *good* thing? Didn't it show how far father and son had come that he would do anything to spare his father any undue worry?

'I didn't want him collapsing, Sophie.'

'I understand. But now he thinks…' She shook her head and tried a laugh on for size.

'Is it all such a lie?'

'What do you mean?' Sophie's heart picked up pace.

'We're an item, aren't we?'

'We are while we're here.'

'Let's not get lost in the detail.'

'Isn't it a bit more than a detail?'

Had she hoped for something more? Had she hoped for a declaration that he wanted more than just a passing fling? She must have been mad… But here they were, stuck in a lie not of her making, and what on earth happened next?

'What happens when we get back to real life, Alessio?' she asked bluntly. 'We can't maintain this fiction. Leonard isn't an idiot. He's going to realise that you made the whole thing up.'

'You tell me that I've made the whole thing up,' Alessio purred, 'but that's not entirely true, is it?'

Without warning he reached to brush the side of her face with his finger, and Sophie shivered at the hot trail left there. Her mouth parted and her eyelids fluttered, and when he placed a butterfly-gentle kiss on her mouth she responded by sighing into his, swept away on a tide of something that was irresistible.

Treacherous fingers laced into his dark hair, tugging him closer, and she felt his smile as he gently drew away—but only a tiny bit. His forehead touched hers, and when he spoke, his breath was warm on her face.

'Who's kidding who, Sophie?' he queried softly. 'This isn't something that's been concocted out of thin air to placate a questioning old man. It isn't an arrangement that we've actively thought up to deceive him into believing in something that doesn't exist.'

'But...'

'Shh...' He briefly placed his finger on her mouth, before removing it, and then he held her head in his hands and looked at her gravely. 'I wouldn't deliver an outright lie to my father, however much it might help towards easing a thorny situation. I would never drag you into pretending something that didn't exist...that was a complete piece of fiction...'

Caught between his hands, Sophie could scarcely breathe, so mesmerised was she by the intensity in his eyes, the warm sincerity in his voice and the urgency of his explanation.

She hated the way her brain seemed to take a holiday when she was near him, and she knew that she should be fighting harder to resist the soft persuasion in his voice. But when she tried to get hold of some vigour, she drew an unhelpful blank.

'We *are* an item, Sophie. We're lovers. And I wasn't lying when I told my father that you're different from all the other women I've ever been out with.'

'You weren't?' Sophie croaked.

Alessio shot her a crooked smile. 'You *are* different. I'd say you're unique…'

Sophie blinked, owl-like, and then recovered sufficiently to get hold of some much-needed common sense.

'So unique that we're not going to prolong this once we return to Planet Earth…' she countered.

For a few seconds Alessio was shaken by the thought that he wasn't entirely sure on that front.

Would they continue what they'd started?

He was so accustomed to having relationships that were defined by the very temporariness of their nature, that he was taken aback to discover that it was different with this one.

At least, it *felt* different.

Maybe he had accepted on some level that they would be destined to meet over time, whether or not they continued what they had.

Maybe in that respect he hadn't got around to mentally predicting the parting of the ways scenario.

At any rate, it was disturbing that he hadn't envisaged ending what they'd begun. At least not in any kind of conscious way. He'd assumed... *What?* What had he assumed? That this would continue indefinitely? Because he wasn't ready to think about her not being there?

Alessio frowned.

'I hadn't thought that far ahead,' he said smoothly. 'Had you?'

'Of course I had,' Sophie answered. 'I'd thought that this was good, but naturally it was going to come to an end. Nothing long term for either of us. A week or two of fun and then we go our separate ways.'

'Well,' Alessio said briskly, 'that line of thinking will have to be put on hold for both of us.'

'How is that going to work, Alessio?'

'It seems relatively straightforward to me.'

'How so?'

'My father is under the impression that this is more than it is...'

He looked at her from under dark, sooty lashes. Her cool agreement with what he'd said should have pleased him. He hated histrionics, and had discovered that women frequently went down that road when it dawned on them that he wasn't for taming. That he hadn't been lying when he'd told them that longevity wasn't in his DNA when it came to relationships.

'That's the problem,' Sophie said, without the slightest inflection in her voice. 'I know you didn't want to stress him out, but I think he would have been okay if we'd been truthful.'

'Not a chance I wanted to take.' He flushed. 'I know what you're thinking, Sophie. You're thinking that I jumped into a lie to protect a father I've barely visited for…for some time.'

There was so much humanity in that admission, from the tone of his voice to the guilty flush that slanted his cheekbones. She felt a wave of tenderness wash through her and her expression softened.

'That's the sound of a guilty conscience talking, Alessio,' she said gently. 'I wasn't thinking any such thing. In fact, I suppose I was rather pleased that you were prepared to go to such lengths to make sure you didn't stress him out unduly…'

'How so?'

Her heart melted further at the quick glance he shot at her, uncertain and questioning. He *wanted* to hear what she had to say. How different was this man from the ice-cold stranger she had confronted not that long ago at his offices in London! A man ruled by his watch, eager to see the back of her and disbelieving of what she'd had to say.

'You've changed. You both have. You and your father.' She gazed at him thoughtfully. 'You might still circle around one another, but the circles are smaller, and there are times when they're not there at all. So I appreciate that you didn't want to jeopardise the bridge that's being built…'

'I'm not sure the situation is really as complex as that—'

'But we're still left with a problem.'

'With one or two upsides.'

'Really?'

'The past few days have stretched me to breaking point, Sophie.'

Alessio shot her a look of pure, wicked charm that made her blood sizzle.

'How so?'

'You know how. Being near you when my father's around...wanting to touch you and not being able to...'

Sophie reddened. Her body began a steady throb. Yes, she knew exactly what he was talking about. Conscious of Leonard's watchful gaze, they had moved around one another, keeping their distance, but those quick glances when their eyes had met had made her blood boil. Sometimes, handing her something or moving towards his father, Alessio would brush against her, and when he did every nerve ending in her body had gone into overdrive.

There hadn't been a single moment during any day when she hadn't been thinking ahead to when Leonard would be safely in bed and she and Alessio could creep into his room like kids playing truant. She'd caught herself drifting off into fantasy land and picturing them together, turned on by images of what they would do once their clothes were off and they were free to touch one another.

The net result?

They'd thrown caution to the winds and taken chances which had landed them in this current mess.

Sophie was ashamed to admit, even to herself, that

still, right now, in this concerning situation, what she really wanted to do was strip off all her stupid clothes, straddle the sexy hunk sitting opposite her and feel him plunge into her wet depths. She wanted to fling herself back and feel his tongue laving her nipples.

She drew in a shaky breath and forced herself back into a position of self-control. 'When we return to England, things aren't going to be straightforward,' she muttered.

'The house should be up and running,' Alessio pointed out. 'Largely. There will still be work to do, but nothing that would impede either you or my father from moving around.'

'You've had updates?'

'And I'm keeping my father in the loop. He insists on being involved in every decision taken.'

'Tiring…' Sophie murmured, momentarily distracted.

'Tiring for him. Utterly exhausting for everyone else. I had no idea he could be so insistent on choosing what shade of paint he wants the hall done in.'

'He hasn't mentioned anything to me…'

'At any rate, by the time we return to the UK…'

'You'll be ready to head back down to London?' she finished for him.

'More or less.'

Alessio found that the thought didn't appeal as much as it should have.

'Things will fade between us. It happens. Relationships burn, then sizzle, then gradually stutter until there's nothing left.'

'That's such a sad way of looking at things, Alessio.'

Wake-up call. Alessio stiffened, reminded of why what this woman and many others called sad, he labelled realistic—because it was realistic to protect yourself from the pain of loss, and if loving came with loss then he was happy to discard that fantasy.

'Let's agree to disagree on that one,' he said, his voice cool. 'Trust me on this. We play along for a bit, have some fun in the process, and in a couple of weeks' time you'll find that telling a small white lie to help an old man out will have been worth it…'

The 'old man', Sophie discovered the following morning, had a spring in his step now that he had been given something to live for.

Since when had he ever admitted to her that he'd been longing to see Alessio involved with a suitable woman?

He had scoffed at his son's love-life, jabbing his finger disapprovingly at all the pictures in those articles he had shown her over the years, but he had never banged on about his son settling down, far less framed his own happiness as being something influenced by Alessio's choices. They'd barely been on speaking terms, for heaven's sake!

Yet now he was heaping praise on the newly outed lovebirds, encouraging them to spend time together and leave him to get on with his recovery, happy in the knowledge that his world was a brighter place.

'This isn't going to end well,' Sophie said worriedly now, as she and Alessio were waved from the door by a beaming Leonard, who had declared himself fit to handle the rest of the work on his house remotely.

They had been discussing the possibility of going on a wine and food tour with a private guide. They would visit the vineyards near one of the lakeside towns and sample the local cuisine, all in five-star luxury. But on hearing of the lovebirds' sudden relationship, Leonard had been only too happy to send them on their way alone. Nothing, it seemed, should stand in the way of their blossoming love affair.

'It'll be fine,' Alessio murmured. 'We have the freedom to enjoy ourselves while we're here. Let's not find ways of downgrading the opportunity.'

He turned to look at her, swivelling her and then holding her in place. In truth, Alessio was happy with the turn of events.

The shock of bumping into his father outside the bedroom door had faded with astonishing speed.

As far as he was concerned, there was nothing not to like about this arrangement.

On every front, it ticked the boxes.

Firstly, he had rescued his father from another possible episode by eliminating a potential source of stress. Hadn't the consultant specifically warned of the dangers of his father worrying to the point where his health would be impacted? Good progress was being made on that front, so why would he jeopardise that?

Secondly, he had legitimised the relationship be-

tween him and Sophie. No more sidelong glances…
no more hot, fleeting brushing of hand against hand.
Now there was positive encouragement to spend time
together!

And thirdly, perhaps for the first time in a very long
time, he could feel the strength of a bond he had thought
perished.

It felt good.

He had relegated his relationship with his father to
a distant holding pen, wherein they co-existed without
any real communication.

Things had been changing on that front ever since
he'd discovered the whole mess with his father's finances.

And now?

Now things had changed even more—and, yes, that
felt good.

'We can do the vineyards another time.' he said.
'Right now, I want to take you to a little village that's
not very far from here. The last time I visited was some
time ago. I want to show it to you… We'll have lunch.
Look at these skies. Bright blue. Cold, yes, but the day
is waiting to be explored.'

Sophie could feel all her urgent doubts ebbing away.

Today he looked devastating, in black jeans and a
thick black rollneck jumper, over which he wore a tan
cashmere coat.

Against the backdrop of colourful houses and ma-
jestic mountains he looked every inch the sophisticate.

Very expensive…drop-dead gorgeous…and thrillingly *all hers*. Sort of…

Her heartbeat quickened.

They were here, weren't they?

Of course this relationship—if you could even call it that—wasn't going anywhere! But just for the moment Alessio had dumped them in this situation and one thing was clear…

She hadn't stopped fancying him.

Close to him like this, she found her head was filled with images of them making love. She thought of the way his fingers felt when they moved along her body, and she couldn't control the soft tremble that rippled through her.

Who was she kidding?

Was she really going to hold his feet to the fire and labour the point about not liking what they had bought into?

He would laugh out loud! Because here she was, and she just couldn't stop herself from responding to him.

Besides, what would be the point of arguing? Leonard believed what he believed, and to undo that piece of fiction now would be cruel.

Maybe Alessio had a point.

They were both adults and they had entered into this with their eyes wide open. Why not just relax and enjoy what had been brought out into the open?

Once they were back in the UK she could focus on thinking of a way out. They *both* could. Because she was pretty sure that Alessio, with his phobia of anything long-lasting, would be anxious to find the nearest exit and scramble through it as fast as he could.

She could start drip-feeding Leonard, hinting that all might not be right in the land of milk and honey.

Old he might be, but he was no fool. He would follow the thread without too much difficulty.

And why wouldn't he?

Anyone could see that she and Alessio couldn't be worse suited.

She was serious…thoughtful…interested in love and marriage and having kids…

He was casual,…dismissive of love and marriage… and into women who were happy to clear off almost as soon as they'd knocked on his front door.

Bolstered by the thought of her sensible way forward, Sophie smiled at Alessio, and her heart filled as he smiled back.

'So…would you like me to tell you where I'm taking you?' Alessio murmured. 'Or would you rather be surprised?'

He slung his arm over her shoulders and drew her against him. She rested her head against his arm and felt utterly content.

'I've never liked surprises,' she mused.

'I get it.'

Sophie felt him angle his head to look down at her as he kissed the crown of her head.

'We have more in common than either of us imagines. I'm not a fan of surprises either. Okay. No surprises, in that case…'

He told her where he was taking her—a little village where he had invested in a restaurant that was now world-class...

The driver who had been booked to take them on the now discarded vineyard tour was rerouted to drive them to what turned out to be a truly stunning village, sitting on the very tip of the peninsula. Under the never-ending milky blue skies Sophie gasped at an exquisite thirteenth-century castle that rose in a series of dramatic turrets, around which was clustered a charming array of shops and boutiques and cafés. The reds and ochres and pinks and pale greens of the buildings gave the place an inviting, cosy feel, even though the fabric of every edifice was imbued with its history.

She wondered whether he'd made this enchanting trip in the company of other women, and felt a spurt of jealousy which she squashed because it was inappropriate.

'If you enjoy coming here so much,' she said pensively, as they wound their way through narrow streets, ending up at the promised restaurant, 'why don't you visit more often?'

'Time is money.'

'You're managing to find the time to be here now...'

'My father would expect nothing less.'

'So it's all about your dad? Why you're here?'

Her voice sounded light and teasing, and she wondered whether she was the only one to register the sting of hurt under the surface.

'There's only so much self-sacrifice a guy is capable of...'

With the restaurant in front of them, and expensively

dressed people walking around them, and the bright blue skies reflecting the mirror shine of the lake, he swivelled her to make her look at him.

'Let me tell you in detail about all the other things we're going to get up to... I'm sure you won't be too surprised by any of it...'

There was one surprise.

After a long, lazy lunch, Sophie found that he'd booked them a room at one of the most exclusive hotels in the small town.

'I promised that I'd show you just how signed up I am to our little charade...' he murmured, in a devilishly sexy undertone.

'We can't stay here for the night!' Sophie gasped, walking into a room adorned in sumptuous deep blues and creams and dominated by the most romantic four-poster bed she had ever seen. 'Leonard—'

'Who said anything about spending the night?'

They spent two hours luxuriating in a hotel where one night probably cost the same as a month's worth of her pay.

This was what a woman got when she became the sole focus of this man's attention. She got luxury and opulence on a biblical scale.

She got envious glances from every woman who walked by.

She got the sort of undivided attention that could make her head swim and make her forget the importance of common sense.

She got a guy committed to a charade he would enjoy

while it lasted but discard when the time came without a backward glance.

She got a guy who had the attention span of a toddler when it came to relationships.

She got the one guy in the world she knew she should never have become involved with but, now that she had, could not detach from.

It was a wildly decadent afternoon, with the banks of ivory shutters closed against the world outside.

It was clandestine and sneaky and thrilling.

She feasted on his nakedness, openly admiring the flex of muscle and sinew and the darkness of his olive skin so defined against her much paler English tone.

She gave herself utterly to him as he explored her body. His fingers were magical as they teased her into a complete meltdown, and the world outside was forgotten under the onslaught of their lovemaking.

They surfaced to strewn clothes, into which they both had to climb after luxuriating in a circular bath that was as big as a swimming pool.

'Now, tell me that wasn't fun,' Alessio purred once they were outside, where the blast of cold sunshine was an unpleasant intrusion.

Sophie slipped her arm around his waist, underneath his coat, and could feel the warm vibrancy of his body… the very body that had taken her to the moon and beyond.

It had been fun.

There hadn't been a second in that bed, with the sounds of real life snuffed out for a couple of hours, that she hadn't enjoyed.

Alessio had said that it was a straightforward situation. He'd told her to trust him—that bridges could be crossed later. Living in the moment would be good for Leonard…it was just one small lie, one tiny reworking of the truth…

They hadn't asked for this situation, but it had happened and it would be fine.

So why did she feel uneasy? Was it because she was inherently cautious? Was there such a thing as *too* cautious? Would loosening up a little rub out her unease?

Did it matter? They were where they were, after all.

It was nearly five in the afternoon by the time they made it back to Alessio's villa, and before they could ring the doorbell Leonard was there, pulling open the door to greet them with a broad smile as he hustled them in.

'Nice afternoon?' he asked.

Sophie reddened and looked away, leaving Alessio to move into faultless conversational mode.

'Good, good, good…very nice.'

They ended up in the kitchen, and Leonard turned to them to say, with satisfaction, that it was time for them to return to England.

'Getting a little bored here,' he said, and beamed. 'Might be old, but the brain needs stimulation and there's not much to be had in these parts. Need to get back to my routine! And you kids…your future ahead of you…you'll be wanting to get back to the hustle and bustle…'

'What about the renovations, Leonard?' Sophie frowned. 'The chaos of the builders…?'

Leonard flapped his hand dismissively. 'I can cope. Besides, I have things to do…'

'What things?'

He tapped the side of his nose and winked at her.

'*Things.* No need to trouble yourself, my dear. You just enjoy having fun with this son of mine!'

CHAPTER NINE

IT WAS A wrench, leaving the villa behind. But Leonard, mind made up, would hear nothing from either of them about staying a minute longer, thus leaving the building work more time to reach completion so that he could be spared the nuisance of returning to renovations still in progress.

He was champing at the bit to get going, and within thirty-six hours Alessio was locking the front door and giving instructions to his housekeeper.

'I don't get it,' Sophie said, when finally they were in a chauffeured limousine, heading from the airfield where Alessio's private jet had landed to Leonard's house in Harrogate. 'He made such a fuss about the work being done, and the inconvenience of having people tramping through his house and ripping it apart...'

This was said in low, whispered tones, while in the front seat, which Leonard had demanded, because his stomach was feeling a little sensitive, he slumbered.

'New lease of life,' Alessio murmured wryly, although there was a hint of an edge to his voice that revealed he wasn't quite as laid-back as he wanted her to think.

His hand was resting lightly on hers. Sophie's eyes drifted to it, and she wondered whether he was already regretting the lie he had told. Was it now dawning on him how problematic it might be to extricate himself from an arrangement he hadn't banked on lasting more than a couple of weeks?

Had reality reasserted itself now that they were back on home soil? It was one thing living in a bubble for a while, but bubbles always burst, and she wondered whether Alessio was now getting to grips with that reality.

'Don't say that,' Sophie said, dismayed.

'Why pretend otherwise?'

'If Leonard has a new lease of life because of this... this lie we've told him, then it's going to be so much more difficult untangling the whole mess.'

'Where there's a will, there's a way.'

'That's just a platitude,' Sophie muttered under her breath.

'Platitudes are a bit like homilies and clichés... they're irritating, but often contain an element of truth.'

'When do you plan on returning to London?'

'I haven't given it much thought.'

'I think it should be sooner rather than later.'

'Explain.'

Sophie turned to look at him and their eyes tangled. For a few breathless moments she succumbed to an unsteady drowning sensation that she knew she had to resist.

'If I need to start working on a way out of this…'
she broke eye contact with Alessio and stared ahead to
where Leonard's head was lolling as he slept '…then
it's going to be easier if you aren't around.'

*Tempting me…thrilling me…making me want to keep
touching you and seeing you and hearing your voice…*

'How so? Alessio narrowed his eyes.

She had her profile to him, and he wanted to tilt her
head, make her look him in the eyes so that he could
read what she was thinking.

The force of his wanting meshed with the force of
his needing. Where did one begin and the other end?

It was disconcerting. It drove all his defences into
gear. But still…

Around this woman, his defences didn't do what
they'd been trained to do.

Around her, he sometimes felt as though his outer
armour had been stripped away, leaving him vulnerable to…

To what?

He didn't know. It confused him, and confusion was
an emotion that he had no intention of tolerating. Confusion equalled weakness, and Alessio knew what if
felt like to be weak, to be helpless. He had been swept
away on a tidal wave of grief after his mother's death.
Too young to navigate those choppy waters, and faced
with a distant father who had withdrawn into himself,
he had been carried along on currents over which he
had had no control.

Of course he had come through those turbulent

times, but he had a very long memory when it came to things like that.

'Well?' he pressed. 'I'm guessing that you have some kind of plan in mind?'

'We're very different people...'

'And?'

'And under any other circumstances there's no way we would have...would have...'

'Say it, Sophie.'

'There's no way we would have ended up in bed together.'

She kept her voice low, although early into the journey Alessio had slid shut the partition separating them from his driver and Leonard still asleep in the passenger seat.

Neither could hear a word, but it still felt weird having this intimate conversation with two other people so close by.

She actually couldn't say the word *lovers*.

She knew that she was bright red, and she guessed that he was probably laughing at her circumspection.

How could you sleep with someone, touch them in the most intimate places imaginable, and then clam up when it came to calling a spade a spade?

Lack of experience.

She'd thought she was tough, having been through a lot growing up, but no amount of toughness had prepared her for a man like Alessio.

She breathed in deeply and held his dark gaze.

'You know that for sure?' he asked.

'Yes.'

'So you think we only ended up being lovers because we happened to be in the same place at the same time?'

'Sort of. More or less.'

'That doesn't say much for the powers of attraction, does it?'

'What do you mean?'

Alessio ignored that question. 'Furthermore, I find it pretty offensive.'

'I don't know what you're talking about!'

Sophie stared at him in dismay. She realised how much she didn't want to hurt him, even though she knew that he was immune to being hurt by anything she said.

His opinion mattered to her.

He mattered to her.

Had her lack of experience brought her to this dangerous point? What was she going to do about it?

Rather, how urgent was the need to do something about it? Just at the moment that need felt pressing.

'How shallow do you think I am?' he asked.

She tried to look down, but Alessio tilted her chin so that she was forced to meet his stare.

'I don't think you're shallow. In fact,' she said with searing honesty, 'you're one of the most complex human beings I've ever met in my entire life.'

Alessio relaxed and half smiled, and Sophie was stupidly pleased that some of the tension had been erased.

'Why did you find what I said…offensive?' she asked.

'I'm not the kind of guy who decides to sleep with a woman just because she happens to be there. I slept with you because you're sexy as hell. You're smart, you're funny, and you're one of the most interesting women I've ever known.'

Sophie smiled back at him. 'Yet, you've known me for a while,' she pointed out gently.

'Have I?'

'I've been working for your father for over two years.'

'You've always been very careful to keep yourself hidden from me.'

'Have I?'

'I've said this before. You've made a point of avoiding me. Why? And don't tell me it was to give me quality time with my father. Things have improved in leaps and bounds between us, but for a very long time, quality time with him wasn't a goal of mine.'

Sophie stilled. They had become close. And as that had happened, as her defences had fallen, he had gained insights into her. He was sharp and he was experienced when it came to the opposite sex. Vague mumbling about avoiding him so that he could bond with his dad no longer held water.

'So, Sophie,' he drawled, 'did you avoid me because I made you nervous? Why would I have made you nervous?' He grinned and brushed his finger across her cheek. 'Maybe even then you were attracted to me…is that it? Was that why my fiery tigress was once a meek and mild little mouse?'

'You have an ego the size of a continent, Alessio,' she told him. But he was flustering her, and she knew that her colour was bright.

'It's a blessing and a curse.'

'Like I said…' her voice was an insistent hiss '…it was never my place to join you and your dad for dinner…or…or come into the sitting room to have coffee or…or brandy or whatever…'

Alessio tilted his head to one side and looked at her for a while in silence, his dark eyes assessing.

'Maybe I'm just not very confident in myself,' she said, breaking the silence to move the conversation on, because his silence was getting under skin. 'I can't understand why you would be attracted to me.'

'Now you know.'

'Still, there are huge differences between us…' She took a deep breath and ploughed on with reality, rather than giving in to the rush of pleasure which was as powerful as an injection of adrenaline. 'And the reason I asked whether you'd be heading back to London as soon as we get back is that I think I can start dropping hints to your father…you know…about those differences.'

Alessio frowned. He'd been basking in the pleasing satisfaction of wondering whether Sophie had always fancied him. He'd been musing on what he might have done had he been aware of that fact.

What if he had known that she'd been casting hot little sidelong glances in his direction?

The woman had practically made herself invisible every time he had made the trip to Yorkshire to see his father. She'd mastered the art of background dressing.

But if he'd known that she was attracted to him, would he have seen beyond her deliberate attempts to play herself down? Would he have zeroed in on what was so obvious to him now? The understated allure was so much more powerful than all the flamboyant peacock parading of the women he usually dated?

Or would he have steered clear of something that had the potential to get complicated?

Complicated women encouraged complicated situations, and Sophie was a complicated woman.

Right now, things weren't straightforward, but what would happen if a passing attraction turned into something more now that they were involved in this charade?

That wasn't something he had seriously considered, because as far as he was concerned they had both started from the same ground zero...

An irresistible attraction...

A craving that couldn't be pushed away...

And an environment where one thing had inevitably led to another...

But what if she had been nurturing a secret attraction to him for weeks? Months? Years, even?

It might be flattering, but it might also be dangerous. What if she started taking this pretend situation seriously?

She made all the right noises, but Alessio was very switched on when it came to hearing women making all the right noises and then discovering that their aspirations had been at odds with those right noises all along.

Disquiet filled him as another little voice shattered his easy assumption that now a potential problem had been spotted it would be no trouble to put it right.

What if attachments began forming, ambushing his usual cool control?

He thought about her when she wasn't around…she distracted him…he'd barely done a scrap of work since they'd gone to his villa…

When he was being logical, he knew that she was probably vulnerable. She had had a lousy life—almost as lousy as his. She been forced into taking responsibility at a time when she should have been enjoying her youth.

He had been forced into a similar situation, but he had been cushioned by money. He had had his chance to toughen up, and since then he made sure to be the one who called the shots in everything.

He'd lived life where she had retreated from it.

At least that was what he'd worked out from everything she'd told him, and from her reactions and the way she was.

She was a woman waiting for love to strike, whereas he was a guy who knew it never would.

But what if some of what she felt rubbed off on him?

Could that happen?

Alessio feared nothing except the weakness of being dependent on someone else—either financially, intellectually or emotionally.

And so he said now, more to get a grip on himself than anything else, 'I think that's an excellent idea.'

'I… Yes… It's as well we…er…think about this as early as possible…'

'To avoid unnecessary complications? Agreed.'

'Leonard must know that we're two people who aren't suited.'

'Of course he does! But, as you well know, people will easily believe what they *want* to believe.'

'Yes. They do.'

'He's desperate to believe that I might finally have found a woman who is…' he looked at her with a curling wry smile '…not built along the lines of my usual dates.'

'But it won't be long before he works out that just because I'm the opposite of those doe-eyed, adoring blondes you like to have draped over your arm it doesn't mean I'm the real deal.'

Alessio grinned. 'How you amuse me with your biting choice of words…'

Sophie blushed. His eyes roved over her face and she reddened even more.

She could see a dark, burning intent there that mirrored hers. Whatever her head told her, she still wanted this man more than was good for her.

She needed him to return to London as soon as possible for a number of reasons.

She needed him to be physically away from her so that she could start learning how to think straight again.

Plus she needed him to disappear so that she could start sowing the seeds of their eventual break-up.

She needed him to go.

She longed for him to stay.

'But of course you're right.'

His eyes stayed on her face, in a lazy, thorough inspection that made her quiver and tremble and think about sex.

'So…'

Sophie blinked and was brought back down to earth as he continued, his voice mild and cool and sensible.

'So I'll check the house when we get there. I've been getting twice-daily progress reports, and every member of that team knows better than to slack off, but I'll still need to make sure things are where they should be.'

Alessio paused before taking the plunge. Because it was always better to be safe than sorry, and already he could feel himself lulled into thoughts of hanging around for longer...taking her to bed...enjoying long nights with her sleeping next to him...

It made no sense. In a short space of time he had somehow become accustomed to semi waking in the early hours of the morning and reaching out to feel her warm, naked body next to him. It had been as pleasing just to feel her warmth as any amount of hectic lovemaking.

'On the financial side, things have moved at speed,' he said. 'I've made a point of discussing everything with my father so that he's kept in the loop...'

'He hasn't mentioned anything of that sort to me. In fact, he's barely mentioned the whole business of the company losing money...'

Alessio grinned.

Their eyes met in shared amusement and Sophie shivered.

'He's adapted fast,' she murmured drily, and Alessio's lips twitched further.

'You think so? I'd say the old man has gone from

ranting and railing to downright having his say to acquiescence in record time.'

They both burst out laughing and Leonard spun round to look at them. He rapped on the partition, which Alessio obediently slid open.

'What are the pair of you cackling about?'

'We're discussing when Alessio is going to head back down to London.'

Sophie sobered up fast, and shuffled a few inches away from Alessio and his dangerously seductive orbit.

'Why the rush?' Leonard's bushy brows pulled together into a frown.

'An empire to run?' Alessio interjected drily.

'Or is the empire running *you*, my boy? No good if it is! Anyway, you can't leave until the day after tomorrow, earliest.'

'Why's that?'

Leonard tapped the side of his nose and said smugly, 'I want to have a little celebration dinner to mark the turning of the tide.'

'Celebration dinner?'

'Nothing fancy, so no need to start fretting! Sarah is delighted to do the cooking, and I feel with everything that's happened...with my health and all those nights of worrying... I would like to do something a little special to mark a new chapter.'

Sophie's mind drifted. Before he'd had to dispatch his housekeeper, Leonard had been all for formal dinners, even if he was entertaining a party of only one friend. He'd enjoyed that. She was pleased that he was returning to his old form.

She was even more pleased to find, an hour later, that the house had taken shape with such efficiency that any disturbances to Leonard's routine would be minimal.

They'd emerged into bleak cold, with the grey heavy skies wistfully reminding her of what they had left behind, where there had been wall-to-wall blue for a fortnight.

Sarah had been waiting for them, shivering in the open doorway, and the three of them had hurried inside, leaving Alessio's driver to bring up the rear with their bags.

It was freezing outside, but the house was warm. The central heating had been updated.

And inside...

Sophie gasped.

Next to her, Leonard was in an equal state of shock.

This proved just how much could be accomplished when you threw money at something.

Gone was the dated wallpaper and the tired paint and the worn banisters and the flooring which had been lovely once upon a long time ago.

Alessio was running through what had been done, and how the workmen had sectioned off the enormous project so that the basics in the main living areas had been targeted for completion first. His father wouldn't notice much more now, as the remainder of the work could be sealed off from various sections of the sprawling old house.

When Sophie slid a sideways glance at Leonard, she noted how impressed he was by what had been accomplished, and his son's smooth delivery of what he'd promised.

How far they'd come from being those two strangers positioned at opposite ends of the dining table, more engaged in their computers and paperwork than in each other!

When all this was over... This charade for Leonard's benefit...

Suddenly Sophie felt the sting of knowing that she would be superfluous.

Father and son would have one another.

The thought of the loneliness of the life she had put on hold hit her with the force of a sledgehammer and she spun away, pretending to inspect a polished new banister, but she could feel the prickle of tears behind her eyes.

'What's wrong?'

Alessio's voice was gentle behind her, and Sophie breathed in deeply before slowly turning to look at him.

Leonard was vanishing with Sarah, excited to see the remainder of the house, booming that he hoped his colour choices had been respected.

'Well?'

Sophie looked up at Alessio. She lost herself for a few seconds in the deep, dark depths of his gaze. This man had stolen her heart, and she knew that she would have to force herself to contemplate a life without him in it.

How would working for Leonard be tenable if she was on constant edgy alert for Alessio showing up? How would she be able to play the part of wise ex-girlfriend still on good terms with the guy who hadn't worked out for her?

'Well, I shall be relieved when this is over and done with,' she said at last.

'What? The renovations? You'll barely notice the presence of the builders. They've wrapped up most of the areas you and Leonard occupy.'

'I mean,' Sophie said briskly, with a glassy polite smile, 'I'll be pleased when this charade we're spinning for Leonard is over. Seeing him here...so happy to be back in his own territory... Well, it puts into perspective the stupid lie we've both told. And now... Now I wish it was all over and done with.' She gave a heartfelt sigh. 'Then I can get on with my life.'

'Meaning...?'

Sophie shrugged. 'Well, I don't think that my position here will still be tenable once we've "broken up", do you?'

Alessio stilled and stared at her with narrowed intensity. 'That's ridiculous.'

Of course it was—for him, Sophie thought. Because he hadn't invested emotionally. Of course *he* would find it easy to pick up where they had left off. He would expect her to be an amicable ex, happy to have dinner with him and his father when he came to visit—which would be a lot more often, seeing how far their relationship had come.

'I don't think I can play the smiling jilted ex.'

'Then feel free to be the one to jilt *me*.'

'That's not going to work.'

'Why not?' Alessio raked his fingers through his

hair and shot her a fulminating look from under his lush, dark lashes. 'I'm very happy to be dumped. At any rate, this wasn't supposed to jeopardise your job, or make your position uncomfortable in any way. Look...' He cast his eye to the doorway, as if in anticipation of Leonard making a sudden stealthy reappearance. 'This isn't the time or the place to have this conversation. Let's park it for the moment. It's late. My father is going to be returning in a minute. But I'm not comfortable with what you're saying. Why don't we wait until this dinner he's having for us tomorrow evening? We can talk after that.'

'I'm not going to change my mind.'

Alessio placed his finger over her mouth and then traced that finger over her lips.

'Shh... Tomorrow...okay? My father eats early. This dinner should be done by eight and we can finish our conversation then.'

Sophie nodded.

Tomorrow evening they would talk, and then she would begin packing her bags in preparation for the long trip back to the life she had left behind.

What difference would a handful of hours make?

Alessio was conspicuous by his absence the following day. He was working and then giving orders to the construction crew, who were busily doing their thing in a completely different part of the house.

And if Leonard seemed a little over excited, what of it?

He had every right to be, with all the stuff happening with Alessio…with the house…with the business.

And when, at five, he disappeared in a flurry of nudge-nudge, wink-wink coyness, Sophie knew that he was simply excited to be entertaining again…with someone preparing his food and dinner formally served in the newly refurbished dining room.

'Be sure to dress up, my dear!' he carolled, before vanishing to his also newly refurbished quarters. 'I've said the same thing to that beau of yours! He's had to go to the office in Harrogate, but he'll be home in time for our little dinner!'

Sophie was putting the finishing touches to her outfit—which was a simple long-sleeved woollen dress and some flat shoes—when there was a knock on the bedroom door.

Alessio.

Tall, commanding…so stupidly good looking…

And deadly serious.

'We have something of a problem,' he opened, stepping into the bedroom and quietly shutting the door behind him. 'Nice dress, by the way,' he murmured, looking at her with rampant appreciation.

Sophie felt a tell-tale dampness spread—the physical manifestation of her arousal—just because he had looked at her.

Her eyelids fluttered and her nostrils flared and she wasn't sure who took a step closer to who. When his arm circled her she breathed him in, and was floored by the warmth of his sexy, familiar body.

She clung.

She didn't want to.

Not when she was trying to grope her way back to the safety of the emotional independence she had abandoned.

But she couldn't help herself.

She felt him back her against the door, tipping her head so that he could kiss her, in a deep, hungry kiss that met her responding passion.

Her hands were all over him, scrabbling to find purchase, pushing under his white shirt which she'd tugged free of his black trousers.

When the first shred of common sense penetrated she let it slip past, because her need for him was unrelenting.

She unzipped his trousers as he shoved up her dress. They were working together, their hands knowing where to go, their mouths melding and crushing any prospect of restraint.

She quivered and moaned very softly as his finger delved between the folds of her soft femininity to find the pulsing bud of her clitoris. She spasmed against his finger, collapsing like a rag doll, as wave after wave of sensuous pleasure rolled over her.

Her fingers dug into his shoulders.

This was good, but she wanted more…needed more. Needed him to push deep inside her so that her whole body exploded.

She tugged him back, and somehow they made their way to the bed, but only barely. She fell back onto the mattress, still fully dressed.

His zipper was still undone and his shirt was flapping, half out, half still tucked into the waistband of the trousers. He eased his trousers off and reached for the thickness of his erection, bulging against his boxers.

There was no teasing…no time for the game of seduction.

No time for getting their clothes off, even.

They fumbled like horny teenagers, and when he sank into her wetness she contracted around him and moved to his tempo, her body bucking, her nails digging into his shirt, her legs wrapped around him even though the dress was still on, hoicked up around her waist.

It was raw and primitive and visceral, and an explosion of mind-bending pleasure that made her want to sob with the joy and satisfaction of it.

'Alessio…'

She looked away as he kissed her neck, and for a few moments they were both lost in the shuddering aftermath of their lovemaking.

Then he heaved himself off her, and turned to look at her before sliding off the bed. His dark eyes were sombre as she shifted and did something to her dress, tugging it down and then retrieving her the knickers, which were hanging off one ankle, kicked aside in those heady moments of lust.

'Sophie… I've just come from downstairs…'

'Why are you looking so serious?' she asked. 'You're freaking me out.'

'We need to go down there, but I'm warning you: this isn't the small celebration we banked on.'

'What do you mean?'

'I mean, Sophie…that he's asked the whole bloody village…'

CHAPTER TEN

SOPHIE HEARD THE babble of voices from the sitting room before they even hit the bottom of the stairs.

She had been galvanised into action the second that contented, utterly ill-advised post-sex lull had passed and Alessio's urgent, serious voice had reminded her that the cold hand of reality didn't include falling back into the sack with him.

There had been no time to shower, but time enough to straighten herself. Still, she felt utterly lacking in composure as she paused to watch Sarah bustling her way towards the sitting room with a tray of appetisers. Behind her an unfamiliar lad in formal black trousers and a white long-sleeved shirt was carrying a similar tray with drinks.

'Leonard's hired *waiting staff*?'

'So it would seem...' Alessio drawled.

'When? Why? He never mentioned a thing... Did he say anything to you?'

'I think he knew better than to let anything slip.' They looked at one another, paused on the staircase, inches apart, their bodies still warm from the ebbing of their lust.

'What's he playing at?' she asked in a high-pitched voice.

But Sophie knew what Leonard was playing at, and she quailed in horror.

When Alessio had said that 'half the bloody village' had been invited, she'd kept her fingers crossed that he'd exaggerated.

He hadn't.

That much was obvious by the noise levels as they neared the sitting room, which was at the end of long corridor and attached to a huge conservatory, where Leonard was fond of napping in his chair with a view of the garden.

Looking through the open door, Sophie paused to take in the scene in front of her. Sarah and her new assistant, with whom she seemed very familiar, were circulating with nibbles and drinks. On the polished sideboard there was a selection of yet more canapés and buckets filled with bottles of wine and any number of non-alcoholic drinks. Towards the back of the room, perched on a padded chair, Leonard was holding court.

There must have been at least twenty people in the room, and most of them she recognised.

Friends from the village…chums he had worked alongside for years…their other halves…the lady who ran the flower shop…

She paled, and yanked Alessio back before Leonard could spot them, tugging him away from the sitting room and into the snug, which was small and private and set to one side of what Leonard referred to as 'the piano room', even though the piano had long vanished from its pride of place. Sold, she reckoned, to help pay bills.

'This is a nightmare!' she whispered. 'All those people!'

Alessio looked at her…at the patches of colour staining her cheeks and the hectic brightness in her eyes and the look of utter horror on her face.

His body was still coming down from the high of having her touch him.

They hadn't been able keep their hands off one another! That being the case, he couldn't see why she was suddenly shrieking in the face of this charade they had concocted.

So what if a few people thought that this was more serious than it actually was? They could bide their time, couldn't they? Why the rush to find a way out? Why begin formulating all the reasons why the situation didn't stand a chance in hell of going anywhere? Why not enjoy what they had?

He sighed with a mixture of impatience and frustration and raked his fingers through his hair. He leant against the wall and shoved his hand in his trouser pocket and frowned.

'I admit it's not ideal that he's invited people over to…to celebrate, but they're here, and there's nothing we can do about it.'

'No, I know we can't turf them out. But, Alessio… this is a disaster!'

'Disaster seems a bit overblown, don't you think?'

'No! No, I don't!'

He didn't understand. He just didn't get it. Sophie was sapped by the feeling of utter defeat.

'Sophie, this isn't the end of the world.'

'You looked pretty ashen when you breezed into my bedroom to tell me,' she shot back with asperity.

'I was taken aback.'

But then we fell into each other's arms, Sophie thought, *and you realised that, hey, continuing the charade might be okay, irrespective of other people knowing...*

In a heartbeat, Sophie knew what she had to do.

She knew how the land lay. She'd always known how the land was going to lie, because Alessio was honest when it came to telling it like it was.

No commitment.

No emotional entanglements.

No risk of love.

Just great sex for as long as they both felt the same.

Sophie knew that she had entered into their arrangement with her eyes wide open, and then she had allowed herself to sink further and deeper into something that had now ended up meshing around her like a net, until thrashing her way out felt like a struggle.

But she would have to thrash her way out. And the only way she could do that was by being honest.

As long as Alessio was aware of the power he had over her physically...as long as he knew that she wanted him as much as he wanted her, and that she found him downright *irresistible*…what would be the impetus for anything to change for him?

For a while he had gone along with her urgency to work their way out. Had he thought that a healthy dose of reality would re-establish his parameters?

She felt as though she knew the way his mind worked. How had that happened? How had bristling in his company, armed and ready for a fight with an opponent she scorned, turned into something so profound that it was as if her soul had somehow melded with his?

And how on earth had it been a one-way journey?

With *her* doing the sinking while *he* just enjoyed what was on offer with the safety of shore always within striking distance?

Inexperience.

She had been able to walk tough and talk tough, but deep inside her lack of experience had made her as soft as marshmallow.

Or maybe she had just found the guy she'd never even known she'd been looking for—the only problem being that he happened to be the wrong guy…

Could she keep making excuses about all of this?

Did she have the strength to stay put and manoeuvre her way out? Plant seeds of doubt in Leonard's head?

How long would those seeds take before Leonard began edging towards seeing what she wanted him to realise?

A month? Two months? Six?

When Sophie thought about a month more of being with Alessio…or two months…or, horror of horrors, *six*…she felt weak and scared.

She would never be able to convince him that their sleeping together would be a bad idea. She wouldn't even be able to convince *herself* of that.

He touched her and she melted inside.

He looked at her and she burned for him.

And he knew it.

And here they were now, with a crowd of people waiting for them in the sitting room, and she could hazard a pretty healthy guess as to what they'd been told.

The prodigal son had returned. Having wandered in the wilderness for years, Alessio was back. And he had saved Leonard's company—had rescued him from the nightmare of an uncertain financial future and everything that went with that.

And the icing on the cake?

He was going to settle down with someone of whom Leonard approved.

The whole situation made Sophie feel faint, but she knew that she only had herself to blame because she had gone along with Alessio's idea with only a token show of protest.

She had accepted the wisdom of his 'tiny little white lie' because it had been easier. With a duvet pulled up around her, in the darkness of the bedroom and still warm from Alessio's body, she had heard the sound of Leonard outside and the thought of him being stressed out by finding them together had been too much.

She had been weak when she should have been strong.

Not that there was much point weighing up the pros and cons and beating herself up about it now.

It was what it was.

Reality wasn't thinking in the abstract.

Reality was dealing with Leonard and his friends, who were probably all waiting with the champagne ready to be poured, eager to find out when they should make room in their calendars for the Big Day.

There was only one thing Sophie knew would work when it came to getting out of this scenario.

The truth.

'Because…?' she said.

'Come again?'

'You said you were taken aback. Why?'

'There's a room full of people. Leonard will have been regaling them all with stories of our heady love affair…'

'Yes, I'm sure he will have been.'

'What's wrong?' Alessio looked at her narrowly and then sighed. 'Look, I know you have doubts about this but, as I keep telling you, we just have to enjoy what we have. And when the time comes we probably won't even have to explain anything to my father.'

Sophie frowned. 'Sorry, I don't understand.'

'Well, think about it…'

He drew her further into the room, and his hand lightly resting on hers made the blood rush to her face. She could feel the heat emanating from his body, and his careless power over her senses filled her with the urgency to say what she knew she had to say.

'Tell me how I should be thinking about this,' she said coolly, pulling back slightly, enough to detach herself from his loose grip, and then folding her arms protectively over her chest.

'When things inevitably begin to cool between us, my father will pick it up. I realise he might try and play ostrich for a while, but he's sharp enough to see when the end comes and by then the process will have been gradual enough for him to deal with it.'

'Because I would have already started warning him of our impending demise as starry-eyed lovers?'

'Something like that. Now, we should go and join the crowd…'

'Not yet.'

'What else is there to say at this point in time?'

Alessio's voice was laced with frustration, and his dark eyes resting on her face were genuinely puzzled. Sophie knew that he had no idea where she was going with her repeated conversations on the same subject.

Alessio was a solution-driven guy. They had jointly agreed on a temporary solution. They had also agreed on the way out they would take and how to deal with damage limitation when the temporary solution was over.

So of course he would wonder why the Spanish Inquisition now? When Leonard and his friends were all lining up to offer their congratulations? When there was a part to be played? Where was the problem when they actually fancied one another so the part was pretty much on point, all told?

For now…

Sophie drew in a shaky breath and managed to look

him steadily in the eyes. 'This just doesn't work for me, Alessio.'

'It's not going to last for ever.'

'And that's where the problem lies.'

'I'm not following you.'

But he was very still, and his dark eyes were watchful. He might not be following her, but he was following the tenor of her voice, and he must know that wherever it was leading was not going to be a destination at which he wanted to arrive.

'I don't want this to end.'

Sophie saw his natural inclination was to glance away, so this time it was she who gently placed her finger on his chin so that their eyes met, so that he couldn't obscure his reaction.

'When I first came to see you at your office, Alessio, I knew that I was coming to see someone I disliked... someone I disapproved of.'

'I know.'

'I thought I'd never like you.'

'Again, you're not telling me anything I don't already know.'

He smiled, a slow, wicked smile that sent her pulses racing. From dislike...to the force of passion. She knew that that was what he was thinking.

He was about to be brought very quickly down to earth by the bucket of freezing water she intended to pour on his beautiful head.

If she thought too far ahead—if she let her mind drift to what would happen when she'd left—then she was filled with cold dread, so instead, Sophie focused entirely on the moment.

'But things changed,' she continued carefully. 'I saw the way you related to Leonard... I saw both sides of the coin and I realised that you weren't the man I'd thought you were after all.'

'It pays never to make easy assumptions,' Alessio murmured. 'Although I can understand why you jumped to the conclusions that you did.'

'And then...' Sophie sighed ready to dip her toes into the churning waters that lay ahead.

'And then...?'

'We slept together. And every single thing changed for me. Not at first. At first, I was just sleeping with a guy I was attracted to. At first, I was doing something I maybe should have done a long time ago.'

'Is this the right time for us to be having this conversation?'

Alessio's voice was rough, a little unsteady, and Sophie wondered whether alarm bells were beginning to ring. *Too bad.*

'It's the *only* time we can have this conversation, Alessio. Don't worry. Your father won't be sending out the search party just yet. You forget—he's under the illusion that we're loved up. He's probably pleased that we didn't bounce down to join the assembled crowd as soon as they started arriving! He probably thinks that you came upstairs to tell me that we had unexpected visitors and then we just couldn't help gazing helplessly into each other's eyes...'

'You're being sarcastic.'

'I apologise. You know that's not like me. But...' She took a deep breath. 'I'll bet you know where I'm going with this,' she said quietly.

'Do I?'

'Of course you do, Alessio. You're the guy who knows the opposite sex inside out. You must surely realise that I've fallen in love with you?'

Of course he knew.

Sophie saw the way he paled. She wondered how fast he would start agreeing with her that the sooner they brought this farce to a close, the better.

'I didn't want to,' she confessed. 'I thought I was immune to a guy like you, because you weren't the sort of man I'd ever had on my list as someone I want to end up spending my life with. And the reason I'm telling you this...'

She waited for a response, but silence greeted her question. For once, Alessio was clearly deprived of the power of speech by the sheer scale of his horror at what he had just been told.

Sophie bit down on the hurt tearing her apart.

'The reason I'm telling you this *now*...' she went on, 'is because I just can't be with you any longer...knowing that what we have is going nowhere. For you, it's all about the hot sex—and believe me, I'm not pointing any fingers, because you never hid the fact that that was the kind of guy you are. But for me...? I want so much more, Alessio. I want to spend the rest of my life with you. I want what your father believes to be true.'

If it wasn't so tragic, it might be funny. His mouth

was half open. His eyes were glazed. His fingers, as he raked them through his dark hair, were shaky.

He was a man in the grip of a nightmare.

'So,' she continued briskly, pulling herself together and saving her sadness for when she was on her own, 'here's what I'm going to do, Alessio. I'm going to go in there and, before this all gets even more out of hand, I'm going to tell your father the truth.'

'Sophie…he's…'

'He's going to have to understand what the situation is. I'm going to be honest. But I'm not going to dump you in anything—don't worry. Then, when I've done that, I'm going to head upstairs and I'm going to pack as much stuff as I can. And then, when I've done *that*, I'm going to call a cab and head to the station and pay my mother a little visit. She won't be expecting me. She'll be really pleased.'

'And my father? How is he going to feel in the face of all this truth-telling?'

'Alessio, it's time I thought about how *I* will cope instead of how your father copes. You'll be here for him. That's the main thing.'

Silence drummed between them, alive and throbbing.

'And,' Sophie added with searing honesty, 'of course I'll keep in touch with Leonard. He's a huge part of my life.'

She waited.

What, Alessio thought, did she want him to say?

'If that's what you feel you have to do, then do it,' he said.

His voice had cooled. There was only one way of stopping her and that would be to promise things he could never deliver.

He liked her. He respected her. He fancied her as he'd never fancied any woman in his life before. But that was never going to be enough. Because she wanted him to love her and he would never love her.

Fear tore into him. Fear of what life might look like without her in it.

He rejected it before it had time to take root.

'You want what I will never be able to give you,' he told her, just in case she'd got the wrong idea…just in case she thought that his silence meant something it didn't.

Just in case he was drawn into thinking that this might be more than what it was. Just in case…

He stood back and shoved his hands into his pockets, and then he watched as she spun round on her heel and headed towards the door, pausing for less than a couple of seconds before leaving without looking back.

Alessio stood his ground.

He stayed put with gritted determination, conjuring up in his head a scene the likes of which he could never countenance.

Over-emotional behaviour…hand-wringing and breast-beating and tears.

No. Not for him.

But for it to all be over…

Sophie's confession rang in his ears.

She had fallen in love with him.

He hadn't asked her to! He'd hadn't encouraged her.

Had he? No. Emphatically not! He didn't *do* love. Love was loss, and loss was something he had scrupulously avoided his entire adult life. He would not sign up to the idiocy of being vulnerable to the whims of someone else. How could you have any control over your life if you foolishly handed the reins to someone else?

Yet she was walking away.

He would never see her again.

The space that opened up at his feet when he thought about that made him suck in a sharp breath, and for a few seconds he was queasy.

Would it hurt to see how this played out? There was no point in trying to stop her, and of course he didn't want to do that.

A declaration of love was a gauntlet thrown down... it was an ultimatum he had no intention of meeting.

About to pour himself something stiff, Alessio instead padded out of the room. He hesitated...drawn to where the assembled guests would be hearing... *What?*

He found out soon enough.

He was rooted to the spot by Sophie's ringing, confident voice.

Leonard had obviously imparted the glad tidings to everyone there that a marriage was imminent. That the prodigal son had returned and was to be married to the perfect woman!

And now Sophie was in the process of gently disabusing them of any such understanding, and Alessio was riveted, struck dumb by her sheer courage and the calm in her voice.

He stood, unseen, and listened for a few moments, his breathing thick, his thoughts in disarray.

Sophie had no idea where Alessio was.

She couldn't think about that just at the moment because she was too busy playing to a rapt audience.

She had done her best to wrest Leonard away from his coterie of friends, but he had waved her aside. He'd been far too busy carolling the joys of his son finally settling down and saying it was *'about time, dammit.'*

And now here she was. She'd cleared her throat and nervously ploughed into a stammering explanation of everything, pushing past the moment when all the excited voices had fallen silent—including Leonard's.

She looked around her.

She could barely meet Leonard's eyes, but she did it because he was really the one she was talking to and she was going to be firm but gentle.

'We did it with the best of intentions,' she said softly, motioning for him to come closer to her...close enough for her to reach out and hold his hand in hers.

Even so, everyone else clustered around her too, and she knew she was also addressing them—like it or not.

'I don't understand...' Leonard blustered.

'I was a coward,' she told him. 'You surprised us, and we rushed into an explanation we thought you would accept because we didn't want to stress you out.'

'*You* weren't the coward! Alessio—'

'He did what he thought was best because that's the kind of guy he is, Leonard. He's a good man. What happened wasn't his fault. It was mine.'

'I'm not getting you, my girl. You'll have to stop talking in riddles.'

Sophie could feel the prickle of nervous perspiration breaking out all over her body like a tingling, uncomfortable nettle rash, making her want to fidget even though she remained calm and composed. At least on the surface.

Inside, she was breaking up.

'I made the mistake of falling in love,' she said quietly, 'and before you jump into any accusations, this wasn't Alessio's fault. He laid his cards on the table from the start. It just so happened that my foolish heart didn't obey the rules of the game.'

'Made the mistake… Falling in love… Wasn't Alessio's fault…'

Alessio had to strain to hear what she was saying, but it was possible because you could have heard a pin drop in the silent room.

He'd imagined an impassioned speech, but he was given instead a quiet, resigned and accepting confession.

And through it all, however she felt after his response to the outpouring of her heart, there was no bitterness in her lowered voice.

Something inside him twisted as the full force of the realisation he'd been hiding from hit him.

It wasn't just a case of her loving *him*.

It was a case of him loving *her* right back.

How had that happened?

And how had he not realised earlier?

The signs had been there. The need to see her…the

peace and contentment he felt when he was with her... the way everything inside him took flight at the sound of her voice... The way she made him laugh and he thought about her all the time.

And yet he had pretended to himself that he was immune to the nonsense of love.

Of course Alessio knew just what he had to do.

But would she have him? Would she even believe him? After all, he was the guy who had been happy to launch into a convenient lie.

Would he be rejected?

Just like that, Alessio knew what love was all about. It was about preferring the pain of rejection to the safety of living in an ivory tower. It was about not having a choice when it came to taking a risk with your heart. It was about opening a door that had been kept locked his entire life.

He walked into the room.

All eyes turned in his direction—including his father's.

Alessio had expected condemnation from him. Instead, there was acceptance. They had both come a very long way, he acknowledged. Bridges had been built, and those bridges were now making it possible for them to communicate with trust and affection instead of suspicion and defensiveness.

And he knew that the woman looking at him, her expression guarded, had played a huge role in building those bridges.

His keen eyes noted the way her back straightened. She was ready to defend herself, braced for confrontation.

He remained standing there and looked at everyone. He recognised a few faces. The rest he would get to know over time.

'I'm sorry,' he said slowly, turning to face Sophie and his father.

'There's no need,' Leonard said heavily. 'Life happens. I should be fuming, but I'm touched that you did what you did to try and protect me.'

'Alessio…'

'Sophie…'

He wanted to reach out for her hand, but she had both of them clasped in front of her.

'I've already explained the situation to your father,' Sophie said dully. 'There's no need for you to play back-up guy.'

'That's not why I'm here.' *In for a penny,* he thought, *in for a pound.* 'Gather around, everyone. It's important you all hear what I have to say.'

'What are you doing?' Sophie asked sharply, and he shot her a wry, self-deprecating smile.

'What I would have done a while back if I hadn't been so damned foolish and so damned stubborn and set in my ways.' He paused, and his dark eyes zeroed in on her confused face. 'You told me you loved me,' he said gravely, 'and I heard you and shut the door on you. It was a mistake. That door…the door that safeguarded my heart…was blown open by you a while back, but I was too entrenched in my attitudes to realise it.'

He glanced across to his father, whose eyebrows were raised, and Alessio threw him a sheepish, wry smile.

'No more little white lies, Dad. The truth now, and nothing but the truth.'

His dark gaze rested on Sophie, and he felt a tug of love and need and want that was so powerful it nearly blew him off his feet.

'Sophie, you got under my skin. And I was kidding myself when I thought that didn't pose any danger for my peace of mind, or my tried and tested self-control.' He breathed in, long and deep. 'I'd spent my life protecting myself from being vulnerable. I'd managed to convince myself that that was a state of affairs that would never change because I would never allow it to. The truth is, Sophie, I stopped caring about my precious self-control within seconds of meeting you... You made me laugh and you made me think and you made me *need*.'

The room had disappeared. The only person in it now was the woman he had fallen head over heels in love with.

'Are you just saying that...? Do you mean it, Alessio?'

'Every word. I was a smug, foolish, short-sighted idiot...'

Sophie smiled, heart bursting as she moved towards him to stare up at his dear, perfect face.

'Now I *know* you're going to regret saying that.'

When she reached to stroke his cheek, he captured her hand in his and closed his eyes to kiss it.

'How could I have known?' he asked in a roughened undertone. 'Known that when love struck my defences would all be washed away like a sandcastle in the path of an advancing tide? I'd been a bystander my entire life and I seriously believed that no one could possibly come along to challenge that. But you did, my darling, and I don't want you to ever stop challenging me. You make me the man I want to be.'

He got down on one knee.

'I have no ring, Sophie, so you might not think much of the grand gesture, but it's made from the very bottom of my heart. I love you more than words can say, and in front of everyone here I'm asking…will you marry me?'

As grand gestures went, Sophie didn't think they could come any grander. Their eyes met and she could see heartfelt sincerity burning in the depths of his dark gaze.

Her heart was bursting. She wanted to pinch herself. Because did dreams like this ever come true?

But he was waiting for her answer.

Everyone was waiting for her answer.

She smiled slowly and said, shakily, 'I can't think of anything I would rather do…'

* * * * *

#4089 THE BABY THE DESERT KING MUST CLAIM
by Lynne Graham

When chef Claire is introduced to her elusive employer, she gets the shock of her life! Because the royal that Claire has been working for is Raif, father to the baby Claire's *just* discovered she's carrying!

#4090 A SECRET HEIR TO SECURE HIS THRONE
by Caitlin Crews

Grief-stricken Paris Apollo is intent on getting revenge for his parents' deaths. And he's just discovered a shocking secret: his son! A legitimate heir will mean a triumphant return to power—*if* Madelyn will marry him...

#4091 BOUND BY THE ITALIAN'S "I DO"
A Billion-Dollar Revenge
by Michelle Smart

Billionaire Gianni destroyed Issy's family legacy. Now, it's time for payback by taking down his company! Then Gianni calls her bluff with an outrageous marriage proposal. And Issy must make one last move...by saying *yes*!

#4092 HIS INNOCENT FOR ONE SPANISH NIGHT
Heirs to the Romero Empire
by Carol Marinelli

Alej's desire for photographer Emily is held at bay solely by his belief she's too innocent for someone so cynical. Until one passionate encounter becomes irresistible! The trouble is, now Alej knows exactly how electric they are together...

HPCNMRA0223

#4093 THE GREEK'S FORGOTTEN MARRIAGE
by Maya Blake

Imogen has finally tracked down her missing husband, Zeph. But he has no recollection of their business-deal union! Yet as Zeph slowly pieces his memories together, one thing is for certain: this time, an on-paper marriage won't be enough!

#4094 RETURNING FOR HIS RUTHLESS REVENGE
by Louise Fuller

When self-made Gabriel hires attorney Dove, it's purely business—unfinished business, that is. Years ago, she broke his heart...now he'll force her to face him! Yet their chemistry is undeniable. Will they finally finish what they started?

#4095 RECLAIMED BY HIS BILLION-DOLLAR RING
by Julia James

It's been eight years since Nikos left Calanthe without a goodbye. Now, becoming the Greek's bride is the only way to help her ailing father. Even if it feels like she's walking back into the lion's den...

#4096 ENGAGED TO LONDON'S WILDEST BILLIONAIRE
Behind the Palace Doors...
by Kali Anthony

Lance's debauched reputation is the stuff of tabloid legend. But entertaining thoughts of his attraction to sheltered Sara would be far too reckless. Then she makes him an impassioned plea to help her escape an arranged wedding. His solution? Their own headline-making engagement!

HPCNMRB0223

Get 4 FREE REWARDS!

We'll send you 2 FREE Books plus 2 FREE Mystery Gifts.

FREE Value Over $20

Both the **Harlequin® Desire** and **Harlequin Presents®** series feature compelling novels filled with passion, sensuality and intriguing scandals.

YES! Please send me 2 FREE novels from the Harlequin Desire or Harlequin Presents series and my 2 FREE gifts (gifts are worth about $10 retail). After receiving them, if I don't wish to receive any more books, I can return the shipping statement marked "cancel." If I don't cancel, I will receive 6 brand-new Harlequin Presents Larger-Print books every month and be billed just $6.30 each in the U.S. or $6.49 each in Canada, a savings of at least 10% off the cover price, or 6 Harlequin Desire books every month and be billed just $5.05 each in the U.S. or $5.74 each in Canada, a savings of at least 12% off the cover price. It's quite a bargain! Shipping and handling is just 50¢ per book in the U.S. and $1.25 per book in Canada.* I understand that accepting the 2 free books and gifts places me under no obligation to buy anything. I can always return a shipment and cancel at any time by calling the number below. The free books and gifts are mine to keep no matter what I decide.

Choose one: ☐ **Harlequin Desire**
(225/326 HDN GRJ7)

☐ **Harlequin Presents Larger-Print**
(176/376 HDN GRJ7)

Name (please print)

Address   Apt. #

City   State/Province   Zip/Postal Code

Email: Please check this box ☐ if you would like to receive newsletters and promotional emails from Harlequin Enterprises ULC and its affiliates. You can unsubscribe anytime.

Mail to the Harlequin Reader Service:
IN U.S.A.: P.O. Box 1341, Buffalo, NY 14240-8531
IN CANADA: P.O. Box 603, Fort Erie, Ontario L2A 5X3

Want to try 2 free books from another series! Call 1-800-873-8635 or visit www.ReaderService.com.

---

*Terms and prices subject to change without notice. Prices do not include sales taxes, which will be charged (if applicable) based on your state or country of residence. Canadian residents will be charged applicable taxes. Offer not valid in Quebec. This offer is limited to one order per household. Books received may not be as shown. Not valid for current subscribers to the Harlequin Presents or Harlequin Desire series. All orders subject to approval. Credit or debit balances in a customer's account(s) may be offset by any other outstanding balance owed by or to the customer. Please allow 4 to 6 weeks for delivery. Offer available while quantities last.

Your Privacy—Your information is being collected by Harlequin Enterprises ULC, operating as Harlequin Reader Service. For a complete summary of the information we collect, how we use this information and to whom it is disclosed, please visit our privacy notice located at corporate.harlequin.com/privacy-notice. From time to time we may also exchange your personal information with reputable third parties. If you wish to opt out of this sharing of your personal information, please visit readerservice.com/consumerschoice or call 1-800-873-8635. **Notice to California Residents**—Under California law, you have specific rights to control and access your data. For more information on these rights and how to exercise them, visit corporate.harlequin.com/california-privacy.

HDHP22R3

HARLEQUIN
PLUS

Try the best multimedia subscription service for romance readers like you!

Read, Watch and Play.

Experience the easiest way to get the romance content you crave.

Start your **FREE TRIAL** at
www.harlequinplus.com/freetrial.